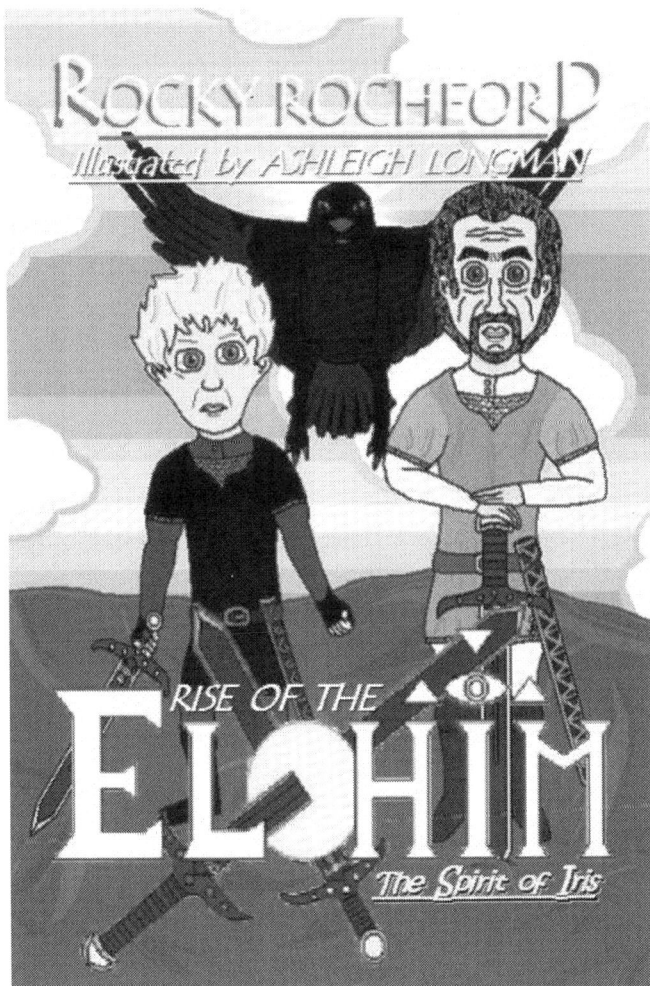

Cover Art:
Ashleigh Longman

Publisher's Note:

This is a work of fiction. All names, characters, places, and
events are the work of the author's imagination.

Any resemblance to real persons, places, or events is
coincidental.

Solstice Publishing - www.solsticepublishing.com

To Alfie Elgar

I HOPE THESE PAGES BRING YOU HOURS OF JOY AND A WONDROUS JOURNEY.

**Dedicated to Ashleigh Longman, my illustrator**

# THE SPIRIT OF IRIS
## *Book 1*
## *Rise of the Elohim Chronicles*

## By: Rocky Rochford
## Illustrated by: Ashleigh Longman

# CHAPTER I:

## *The Storm*

*"As long as our hearts are ruled by hate, we will always be at war, but as long as we have love to direct us, we will never give up!"-Master Mako of Iris*

\*\*\*

Since the dawn of the time, war has always been present, be it a great conflict on a battlefield, or something more personal; the battle we face with ourselves. In every world, history is filled with war, chaos, and destruction. The planet of Oceania was no exception for a great war loomed on the horizon.

Oceania was a world of islands both great and small, each with its own variety of races and species. The islands became realms, and the realms became unified. Oceania flourished.

Then one year a great storm swept down and ravaged the world. A storm like no other, a storm that was alive but brought forth nothing but death and destruction. A storm that was just the first wave of an invasion. A storm that didn't just carry the Dark Ones, but *was* the Dark Ones.

With fear in their hearts, open war broke out between all men as blood spilled on the plains of battlefields. The storm disappeared as quickly as it came, but left the skies filled with darkness.

With men distracted by raging conflicts, a new enemy came slipping through the chaos. One unlike the races of Sancti had ever known. They were beings of pure darkness who desired nothing less than the ultimate reign of terror, supreme power, and rivers of blood. One by one, the Realms fell into the hands of the Dark Ones.

In an effort to save their world, the people joined,

forming a truce to take on those truly responsible for the true devastation of their world. Rising up against the Dark Ones, the united warriors stood successful, weakening them in number and strength, driving them below ground.

The warriors feared evil would one day rise again, so the Watchers were created, a clan of warriors to watch over the Realms of Oceania and protect them. Tyrants would rise, accumulating power only to fall at the hands of the Watchers, the descendants of the warriors who had vanquished the Dark Ones.

Over the centuries, the Watchers continued to thrive and safeguard, always keeping watch, waiting for the darkness to rise so they could drive it back again.

The centuries passed, and rumors of the Dark Ones' return began to surface. It was time for the Watchers to act, but due to the progression of time, the vigorous training and the selection processes, the Watchers had become a mere shadow of their former selves as now only a handful remained. More were desperately needed.

With the return of the shadow threat came stormy times, bringing with them change; change that started small and grew to loom large.

This is the story of a young warrior living on the Isle of Iris in the Mares Realm. The story of Zach and his effort to save the world.

# CHAPTER II:

## *Message from the Sky*

**D**ark clouds covered the sky as droplets of water fell hard and fast on the Isle of Iris. The rain soaked the long, vibrant green blades of grass that covered over half the island's landmass. With a beach, concentrated to the eastern side, consisting of rocks and sand, the rest of the island was laden with rocks, stones, and boulders.

The island itself was one and a half miles long and less than a mile wide. Once shaped like an eye, thanks to decades of erosion and landslides, the island had changed dramatically, now smaller and rectangular in size.

Most of the island stood one hundred meters above the surface of the sea. The beach led up to the rest of the island via a rocky slope that slithered snakelike up the cliff face to the rest of the island.

The highest point on the whole island was the Watcher's Summit, resting atop the peak of the dormant volcano that had given birth to the island. Erect in the centre stood a two story wooden house, built centuries ago from the trees growing on the island.

On this dark night, as the rain continued and the weather seemed to be getting worse, a lone figure stood on the summit, wielding a sword as he slashed out at the wooden targets he had built. He was soaked; his violet colored tunic and white tights clung tightly to his body. The man stood five feet nine inches tall with graying black hair, and a bald spot on the back of his head. A jet-black goatee marked his chin, topped off by a black, bushy moustache.

The aged swordsman of Iris was the sole human inhabitant on the island, and it was not because he chose to live like this. Tradition and protocol dictated a life of solitude, unless a child of worth made their way to the island. Taking another swing, the swordsman struck his wooden man-shaped target again. The lone man of Iris was the chosen Guardian of the Island and one of the last few remaining Watchers in modern times. For a long time he had served as the Iris Watchman, the most skilled watchman in all of the Mares Realm. His duty was to discover and educate all future guardians, teach them the Watcher's Code and train them into highly skilled warriors.

Taking another swing, the swordsman struck his target again.

Swinging his weapon again, the Guardian of Iris was growing weary, not because he was feeling tired from four hours of arduous training, but because his age was beginning to catch up with him. He may have looked like he was in his late forties, but in reality, he was much older. As much as he wished to stop, call it a night, and go to bed, the Guardian wouldn't allow himself to; instead, he willed himself on as he continued to swing. He was cold, tired, and hungry, but still he fought on, battling through his rumbling stomach, craving for anything to eat, and his aching muscles, crying out for a break. This was the way of the Guardians, the Watchers. Even at their weakest, their most exhausted, they were required to give their best. Less than total commitment was not acceptable.

This Guardian, a man who had taught so many, had spent the last twenty-three years in isolation, living without another person to talk to. His only friend was a loyal and dutiful raven, but on this miserable night, things were about to change.

Even with the sounds of rain pelting the earth and his sword repeatedly striking wood, the bearded warrior could still hear a single caw as a bird, off in the distance, called out. He paused in mid-swing and turned east.

"Izal! Is that you?" The Guardian spoke in a strong, powerful, baritone voice. Deeply masculine and authoritative, it was full of wisdom from years of experience.

"Izal?" he repeated, calling out to his feathered companion.

*Caw!*

The man turned again, facing north. This time he had definitely heard a bird calling out; he was positive his mind was not playing tricks on him.

"Izal, I can hear you, my friend! Where are you?" He called out into the night, not hoping but knowing his winged friend could hear him.

*Caw!*

Again, a bird called out, but this time it landed beside its master.

"Izal! I'm so pleased to see you!" the swordsman exclaimed, as he turned to face the four-foot tall raven and reached out with his free hand to stroke his pet.

Izal enjoyed this display of affection from his master. It had been two years since they'd last seen each other.

The two had parted ways at the end of a special ceremony, just as the code dictated. Izal's return could mean one thing and one thing only.

"Izal, am I dreaming?"

*Caw!*

The raven looked into the eyes of the Guardian before its own eyes turned green, shining like emeralds as it began to speak telepathically.

*No, Master Mako, you are not dreaming!*

He was stunned.

"Your return can only mean one thing!" Mako exclaimed.

*Yes, Master, there is a boy on Dead Man's Beach.*

Without another word, the winged creature took flight, toward the silvery moon, heading east.

# CHAPTER III:

## *The Flight of Iris*

As he watched his friend go, Mako's grip tightened on his steel-forged long sword and he let loose an upward diagonal strike, starting from his hip and ending with hands raised higher than his head. The sword slashed down and was deposited into its two-colored sheath, hanging on his left side from his black leather belt.

A flash of lightning lit up the sky, briefly illuminating Mako, who closed his eyes for a second. When he opened them, his almond colored eyes burned with life. Without any warning, he started to run.

Mako's steps were met with the sounds of the rocks sliding and crunching beneath his feet. Neither the rain nor the terrain would deter him from what he had to do so he maintained his pace and continued running toward the easterly ledge. Upon reaching it, Mako leaped, sailing through the air, flying forwards three meters before he started to fall, landing on the sloping incline of the volcano. Like every other time before, he landed on both feet, and slid down the mountain's ramp.

Being as high as it was, going down the ramp was the quickest way down the volcano. Dangerous, but quick.

Halfway down the slope, Mako could not help but let his mind drift off, losing it to the past as he thought about the number of lives the island had claimed. Many a Guardian had lost their lives during training or fighting wars that soaked the Isle of Iris in blood, as the Watchers engaged ferocious beasts in battle. The Isle of Iris had seen a lot of good, too. Many a warrior had aspired to greatness lived joyful lives and, in some cases, they had even found love.

Master Mako quickly had to regain his focus. He was fast approaching the end of the stone ramp at the base of the volcano. Any second now and he'd need to turn fast and hit the man-made ramp. At his current speed, he'd run straight into the Nogmal trees, a rare tree that only existed in the Mares Realm.

It was a fast growing tree, growing at a rate of ten-feet a year, and luckily, it was a very reliable source of wood. Many a sword and shield had been made from it, as well as handles for farming implements, houses, bridges and many other things. The wood was very strong, sturdy, and stayed dry in the wettest conditions, so it never rotted. Nogmal wood lasted forever; its hard exterior was even fire resistant, which is one of its more negative qualities.

They grew to a height of seventy-eight meters, reaching maturity within twenty-four years, and growing to a width of two meters in diameter. They were dark brown in color. They grew out half as much as they grew upward, their branches shooting out in all directions. The tree was armed with many spiky thorns, ready to puncture any fool who would run into it, stabbing its prey to death. This was exactly the fate Mako had in store for himself if he did not make the ramp.

His reaction time was as perfect as it ever had been; he deviated to the ramp with no problems and used his current acceleration to charge up the wooden one made from Nogmal wood, and leaped into the darkened sky. Unlike his earlier leap, this time he really took flight as all the extra momentum from his slide down the volcano aided him, taking him, briefly, to a world above the trees.

This was one of the things that made up a true Watcher; it didn't matter what you were. You could be human, wood elf, ogre, mermaid or any other being that took on the trials of the Watchers and participated in the intense training. All of that and anything you had achieved or could achieve was worthless. You could be a Watcher who saved the world a countless number of times and it still would be insignificant if you couldn't abide by one of the Watchers most important rules:

*To uphold all that is good, a Watcher must learn to be great.*

There were many good Watchers, but not many great ones; two different classes. A good Watcher was a warrior with limitations; a great Watcher was a true Guardian, a warrior who believed anything and everything was possible, so was not limited. One thing a great Watcher was not, however, was mortal, for they were much more. They were the living embodiment of all that was good and were a symbol of hope. Master Mako was the rarer kind, a true Guardian, a great Watcher.

Still flying through the black sky, Mako began to drop, falling to the world once more, and landing on an upper branch of a Nogmal tree closest to him. He leaped to another branch on a smaller tree before repeating the process, bouncing from one tree, to a smaller one. Upon each landing, the branches would shake and shiver, but never break. They remained intact as the bright green leaves with the rounded cloves of three drifted off, lazily floating to the earth below.

Mako continued to leap from tree to tree, only to pause when he reached the end of the tree line, but he did not stop for long. Instead, he only waited for a second before he hurled himself forward, jumping from the last branch on the last tree and into the air for the last time.

From this point onward, the only thing below Mako was Dead Man's Beach, the lowest point on the whole island. Out of all the beaches in the Mares Realm, Dead Man's Beach was also the worst. Only a small portion of it was sandy; the rest was littered with a vast number of stones, millions of them, making up most of the beach.

Along with the many rocks were large, sharp boulders ready to impale anyone who was foolhardy enough to jump from the top of the cliff.

Mako had different plans. As he fell, he pursed his lips and blew, releasing a shrill drawn out whistle that carried in the open night sky, through the rain, and continued to carry until it reached its intended target. Mako's winged friend was high up among the clouds. The moment the raven heard his summons, it dipped its head and commenced a breathtaking dive.

Izal hurtled down to the beach, to his trusted friend, falling toward death. The faithful raven swooped so close that the wise Mako was able to reach out with a steady hand and clutch a single leg. At the moment of contact, Mako's grip tightened dramatically

Even though only one hand held onto the one leg, his strength secured him and prevented him from falling as his avian ally flew him to safety, not even struggling under the duress of the weighty load it now bore.

Izal flew Mako to the sandy area of the beach before he released his grip on his companion's leg and dropped the remaining fifteen feet. He landed on his feet with a soft thud, surviving the Flight of Iris once more.

It was a journey that had taken the lives of over thirty potential Watchers. Some had been young students eager to prove themselves, whereas others were more trained and all too confident, believing themselves superior and no longer in need of any further skill development. Many had come and gone, but now Mako was the only one left, the last surviving Watcher to accomplish the Flight of Iris. The rest had all perished a few from old age and the rest? They died with honor as they each met their end in battle.

# CHAPTER IV:
## *The Boy in the Basket*

Standing on the beach, soaked but unaffected by the cold, Mako scanned the shore, searching for the child his trusted friend spoke of.

"Izal!" Mako called out into the night.

*Caw!*

The bird's reply was inaudible, for the moment, the avian let loose its cry, thunder had roared, releasing a deafening boom.

"Izal!" Mako called out again, this time even louder.

*Caw!*

Once again Izal made his cry, but unlike the last time, Mako was able to hear him. He held out his left arm, keeping it nice and steady before pursing his lips together and whistling.

Flying thirty meters above Mako, Izal heard the whistle and plummeted to the beach below. Even in the dark, Izal had perfect vision. He saw the extended arm and understood its intention. The raven flew gracefully and landed ever so carefully on Mako's arm, so gently that not even one of his talons pierced Mako's skin.

*You called for me, Master?* Once again, Izal's eyes were green as he spoke telepathically.

"Yes, I did. You spoke of a boy." As he spoke, Mako stared into the eyes of the bird sitting comfortably on his arm.

*That I did.*

"Take me to him." Mako commanded.

Obediently, Izal took flight once more, being ever so careful as to not part flesh from bone as he released Mako's arm.

Heading in a north-easterly direction, Izal did not fly at his full speed, but slow enough for Mako to still see him in the dark and be able to follow.

Mako chased after Izal, the sand crunching beneath his feet before he leaped up onto the nearest boulder. Due to all the rainfall, the surface of the rock was very slippery, but Mako did not slip. He maintained perfect footing as he leaped from one rock to another. He voyaged onward, maintaining his pursuit of his friend.

*Getting slower, Master?* Izal teased.

"Who are you calling slow?" Mako replied before he urged himself on, willing his body to move faster.

Now he was moving twice as fast and leaping twice as far. This was another skill of a true Watcher--the ability to summon great strength, speed, and stamina when it was needed most, whether in the middle of battle when they were at their weakest, or when they were exhausted. Mako was very tired and very determined.

As he ran and leaped repeatedly, his breathing was slow and controlled, in through his nose and out through his mouth, but inside his chest was a different story. His heart was beating at a rate of eight beats per second, so fast and so hard that Mako felt like it was going to explode, but he knew better.

"Do you see the boy yet?" Mako whispered. He knew full well that no matter how loudly or quietly he spoke, Izal would hear him regardless. Mako could feel the raven's presence in his mind.

*Caw!*

No words this time, just a sound, but for Mako one sound was more than enough. The gentle call was worth one hundred words. Mako understood its message loud and clear; Izal was with the boy.

As he leaped from one last rock, he landed back on the stony beach. Ten meters in front of him, he could just make out Izal standing beside a wicker basket.

That was unusual. Everything wooden in Mares was made out of Nogmal wood. That could mean only one thing--the basket was from a whole other Realm. The basket and its occupant had travelled a long way to arrive at Iris.

Mako could now easily see inside the wicker basket. Sleeping blissfully, snuggled up in a wool blanket, lay a peaceful baby. He wasn't chubby like most babies, but lean due to not having eaten in quite some time. His skin was pale and bright blonde ringlets of hair framed his face. Mako wondered what color his eyes were.

Mako turned to his feathered friend.

*What is it?* Izal asked.

"The basket, it's made from..." Mako has no time to finish his question as Izal chose to interrupt him.

*Wicker.*

"He's travelled a long way to get here." Mako commented.

*Look in the basket.*

Mako did as suggested. Tucked into the blanket was a thin, long glass bottle, similar in shape to a bottle of wine. Inside it was a single piece of parchment.

Very carefully, Mako reached in and pulled it out. He removed the cork.

*Pop!*

Sticking a single finger into the opening, he caught hold of the parchment and succeeded in digging it out.

*What is it?* Izal asked as he watched Mako unroll the document and study it.

"A letter."

*What does it say?*

"Just a second." Mako gazed intently at the document; it wasn't written in Mari, the language of the Mares realm. Instead, it was written in Algean, a language Mako had not read or heard spoken in quite a while. He needed a moment to recall it before he could translate it.

With knowledge of old coming back to him, Mako translated the letter with ease, reading it out loud so Izal could hear.

> *To whoever finds me,*
> *My name is Zach. I was born in the Month of Easter, nearly two full moons ago and I have travelled far. I am a child of the Algean Realm, from the village of Mantos on Mantos Island.*
> *As is the custom, as I am the first born child in my family, my parents obeyed the code in the hopes that I'd reach the lands of the Guardians and learn their ways.*

# CHAPTER V:

## *Children of Tormenta*

Mako put the letter down and tucked it back into the basket. He knew of Mantos Island. He'd been there twice; once when he was very young and the second time was a couple of decades later when he found himself participating in a quest of the utmost importance. That was a long time ago now, but it was the last journey he had undertaken. The last quest he'd engaged in before reaching his adventure's gripping, climatic end. When it was over, he returned to Iris hadn't left since.

*This child's arrival means only one thing.*

"Yes, training begins again." Mako turned to the raven and observed him.

*True...*

"I sense a 'but' coming," Mako replied.

*...but it also means that one of the prophecies has now come to pass.*

"Prophecy?" Mako asked as he glanced back down at the little baby.

*Think back.*

Mako allowed his mind to wander backward, reaching the code mentioned in the letter.

The code, widely known as the Chosen Law, came into being six centuries ago and was enforced in seven of the eleven Realms of Oceania; Algean and Mares being two of them. The Chosen Law was determined by Watchers, as a means of rooting out the potential for stronger and more highly skilled warriors, instead of just training every child they took in. Many students quit on them, giving up because it was too arduous. As for the ones who didn't quit, a number of them had died from their training or from participating in a series of deadly trials.

So the Watchers of that time made a law for a new training and selection process. They would be given up by their families and taken under the wing of the appointed Guardian of the Realm. Realms could have any number of islands, and to each was appointed a Watcher. Nowadays, their numbers had dwindled so much that only a handful of islands had Watchers.

Also, to every Realm there was one island that was designated a Guardian island, home to Watchers like Mako; the Guardians charged with the duty of training the future Watchers, responsible for the entire Realm. Back when the Watchers brought forth their new law, the Guardian of each Realm would sail from island to island, taking the first-born children from their families and bringing them back to their chosen island to train. The problem with this was that once training started, a few months later the Guardian would have to set off once again, in search of children to train.

The Watchers then decided that to solve this problem, the Guardian of the Realm was to remain on their island for the sea was a very dangerous place and many met their end on the water. It was declared an unnecessary risk, so the Guardians would stay ashore, charged with the task of being forever present to train their students.

As for potential disciples, parents would send their children off however they saw fit; floating them out to sea in baskets, on rafts or in boats, in hopes that the currents would carry them to the islands of the Guardians.

Many children after being sent off were never seen again, but the ones who did finish the journey, the ones who survived the trials and hardships of the tide, the trials and hardships of the training, eventually grew up to become accomplished Watchers. Mako had seen a fair number of children who had made their way to the Isle of Iris and had taught them, but it had been quite some time since he had a pupil to educate.

With a quick shake of the head, Mako returned his thoughts back to the present, only to then allow his mind to dart back, scanning his vast memory for the prophecy Izal was referring too. Mako wasted no time at all in going over it.

The prophecy dated back to a hundred years after the Chosen Law came into being. The teaching Watchers learned that students hailing from further away, from a different realm, were different from students who came from neighboring Islands. For some reason, children who came to the tutors from more distant, different realms all seemed to be stronger, smarter, quicker, and easier to train.

The Watchers believed that a child who had travelled from Realm to Realm by the currents of the seas would face more perilous dangers and be at more risk than an infant who would voyage by ship from island to island. Therefore, they believed that these chosen children were under the protection of the Goddess Tormenta, their one deity. The chosen came to be known as the Children of Tormenta and grew up to become greatest Watchers to ever live. They were the true vanquishers of the Dark Ones.

Mako himself knew a lot about the Children of Tormenta; he was one, born in the Abaran Realm and journeying across the oceans until, at long last, he washed up on the Isle of Iris. He became one of the greatest Watchers to date, the last out of twenty-six chosen infants; the last, that is, until Zach.

It was in times of peace that the Watchers learned that upon the arrival of a Tormenta's Child, within the years that followed, Darkness would rise up once again, attempting to plunge the world into a new age of shadows, and they also learned that the same Tormenta's Child would play a huge role in the Dark One's downfall. It was in that sphere of knowledge that the prophecy was made:

*Come the arrival of the chosen, comes the arrival of*

*the impending Darkness.*

Mako looked to Zach who was still sleeping soundly. Then he turned his concentration and his eyes to his faithful companion.

"Darkness is coming." Mako's eyes hardened as he spoke.

*Yes, it seems the Shanzi will be making their return.*

Mako winced when he heard his friend say the word "Shanzi." It was a word all Watchers knew. It was a word, a language, and a race. Shanzi were the Dark Ones; it was their true name. In every language spoken in all of Oceania, Shanzi was the same word. When translated, it meant 'shadow'.

"I just hope this young lad can live up to the prophecy; a lot depends on it." As he spoke, Mako could feel the rain hitting him faster and faster, the downpour increasing.

*Teach him everything you know, that's all you can do. The rest will be up to him.*

"You're right as always, my friend."

*The rain is getting worse, as is the storm. We should head inside,* Izal told Mako, imploring him to head for home.

"You're quite right. Any chance of a lift?" Mako asked as he scooped up the basket and holding it between his body and one arm, leaving the other free.

Instead of answering Mako's question, Izal chose to leave it unanswered as he began to flap his wings and rise.

*Grasp tightly.*

"Thank you, my friend," Mako said with joy and reached to catch the raven's leg. He made sure his grip was strong before Izal powered his way high up into the sky, soaring above the beach before ascending above the volcano. As Mako's home came into sight, baby Zach continued to sleep.

# CHAPTER VI:

## *The Start of Things to Come*

Although it was now past midnight, Mako was still awake and seated on a stool by a square wooden table positioned against the wall.

The first floor of Mako's two-storey home was a great room, a combination of a kitchen, dining, and sitting room with a stone fireplace. Fierce flames roared in it, burning the stubborn Nogmal wood as well as they could.

If the wood was just cut into a few large pieces and then placed inside the fireplace, then it would not burn. But when the log was cut into many smaller pieces, exposing its softer and more flammable pith, it became usable as fire wood. It was a very slow burning wood so it helped to have a load of leaves on hand to feed the fire.

The kitchen area of the room was made up of a wooden work surface that ran along the eastern wall. The work surface was home to three units, complete with drawers, doors, and handles. The units housed Mako's food, crockery, pots and pans, and the drawers contained his cutlery.

Two units were mounted to the wall in the kitchen above the work area. These were placed so that a clear work area sat between them. Here Mako kept a pot full of water and a sponge, which he used to wash his dishes. Next to it was a wooden chopping board, and knives, pots, and bowls in need of cleaning.

Over on the west side of the room was the dining area. Mako sat here, a bowl of soup before him. This wall held a collection of souvenirs gathered during his lifetime. There were wooden and metal shields, broadswords, long swords, war hammers, arming swords, axes, masks of skulls, and stuffed animals. There were even a number of hand-drawn pictures depicting certain events of his long life.

At the juncture of the west and south walls, there were two windows covered by long, thick, linen crimson curtains. Nearby was the door to the outside. In addition, two chests sat on the floor, containing a variety of weapons, currency, gold, and an assortment of jewels.

More pictures and assorted furniture completed the décor. Baby Zach's basket was on the floor near the fire but not too close, the child still sleeping, lulled by the warmth.

Sitting closer to the fire was Izal; his feathers were drying in no time. To his right was a wooden rack, which had draped over it Mako's soaked tunic, his wet boots on the floor before it.

"How's the fire treating you?" Mako asked, as he reached for his bowl of soup.

He had changed into a violet tunic and, like most of the time; his sword was once again in its sheath, resting by his hip. He dipped his spoon into the soup and raised it to his mouth. He felt good being both warm and working his way to being well fed.

*It's good, my wings are almost dry.*

"Good, then maybe we can talk," Mako said between slurps.

Izal beat his wings and flew over to the table, landing on one of the stools.

*Yes?* Once again, Izal's eyes were green.

"The child is very young."

*They always are.*

"I doubt we'll have enough time to train him," Mako said.

*We'll?* Izal asked.

"I will need your help with this one. I have the feeling the Shanzi will be coming soon, sooner than they ever have done before."

*What makes you say that?*

"The storm. You've seen what it is like out there. It's been like that every night for the last fortnight."

*Yes, I've noticed that.*

"It doesn't feel like a normal storm, it feels like..."

*Something more?* Izal asked.

"Exactly. It feels like Darkness itself is in it."

*You think the Shanzi will be making their arrival via the storm?*

"I do. They did before. Plus, with the arrival of Zach, that's all the proof I need. I believe the Shanzi's presence will be known within a year or two."

*Then that's no time at all.*

"I know. By the time Zach will be ready, *if* he'll be ready, the Shanzi will have a foothold on the world. They will have at least two realms under their control."

*Hence the reason you require my aid in his teaching. You intend to teach him harder and faster than any Watcher has ever been trained.*

"Exactly right, my old friend." Mako grinned as he put his bowl back down on the table, still containing some soup. He reached for the loaf of bread on the table and broke off an end.

*No one has ever been trained like that.*

"I know, but we don't really have the time for the normal manner of teaching." Mako dipped his bit of bread into the soup, and ate it.

*Then I will help you in every way I can.*

"Thank you, Izal."

*I hope he's strong enough.* Izal couldn't help but feel very concerned.

"I do too," Mako admitted between mouthfuls.

Both man and bird glanced over at Zach. The child was still oblivious to the world, dreaming.

*What do you think he's dreaming about?*

Mako got up from his stool and walked over to the

31

boy, kneeling down beside him. Zach had pushed his blanket off in his sleep. Mako gently and carefully retrieved it and pulled it over him.

"I have no idea, but I hope it's of something good because if I'm right and the Shanzi do come, if this boy is not ready, then the world as we know it will become a never ending nightmare."

*Then we will not fail in his training,* Izal said before coming over to join the man and the boy.

"In the morning I will need you to take flight."

*And go where?*

"Everywhere. I need you to deliver a message to the other Watchers for me," Mako said.

*A message, saying what?*

Mako went to the wooden table by the fire. He grabbed a piece of parchment and a quill. Dipping the quill in an inkpot, he wrote out a message, and let the heat from the fire dry it. Then he rose, note in hand.

"Saying this."

Mako held the parchment up so that Izal could read the message:

*The Shanzi are coming. Be ready! - Master Mako, Mares Guardian of the Realm, Isle of Iris*

# CHAPTER VII:

## *Sun, Sea, Sand & Shanzi*

Two years had passed since Mako and Izal discovered the baby Zach. He was now a lively toddler with blond curly hair that was always messy and intelligent blue eyes full of strength and determination. He was chatty, speaking a language of gurgling and cooing. He always wore a cheeky grin and was forever getting into mischief. Whenever left unattended, little Zach would waste no time in wandering off on his own. His tutors couldn't look away for even a second; a second was all it took for Zach to crawl away, putting as much distance between him and his minders as he possibly could.

At first, he would only make ten feet before he was caught, but as he got bigger and stronger, he would get even further. On a number of occasions, Mako and Izal would have to search the entire island to try and find Zach, all because he would crawl and crawl tirelessly. Sometimes he would be found down on the volcano's slope or playing on Dead Man's Beach. Then there were the times that he was found among the Nogmal trees. He was a child who brought his two caregivers a lot of stress and worry.

Most recently, Zach had taken to climbing, climbing up anything he saw. It didn't matter if it was Mako's legs, a table, a stool, or even climbing onto Izal's back, wanting to go for a ride. On some days he even attempted to climb up Mako's house, but his favorite thing to climb was the Nogmal trees. He took great joy out of scaling them, and had no fear of it doing so either for Zach hailed from the island of Mantos, where the people were well known as people of the trees. Even though they were excellent fishermen and highly experienced free divers, the people of

Mantos had an affinity for the forests. They were tremendous tree-climbers and practiced archers capable of making shots no other could – a great natural ability to possess for a Watcher in the making.

Mako took this into account and taught him to work with wood. As well as being able to fight, strategically plan, and speak the many languages of Oceania, Watchers also had to know how to build and how to make wooden swords and shields as well as high quality bows and arrows. They needed to know how to build houses, furniture, and much more. They also learned blacksmithing, thus enabling them to forge some of the finest weaponry made in Oceania, as well as great shields; the education of a Watcher trainee was diverse and thorough.

Mako spent the majority of his time fixing up his house, and mending his little fleet of boats, which he kept hidden in a concealed cave down by Dead Man's Beach. He was also busy making a large quantity of wooden targets, which Zach would soon be destroying once his physical training began.

Izal had spent the first eight months of the two years that had passed, flying from island to island. Some Watchers were easy enough to locate, but some had taken to the seas or were on an adventure of some kind. Island to island, realm to realm, Izal persevered and located them all, travelling the entire world before making his return to Iris.

Home again, Izal turned to spending his days being a minder to Zach, watching him whenever Mako was unable to. As vigilant as the raven was, Zach was always able to make his escape.

On this summer's day, the sky was clear of clouds and the sun sat high up, shining bright as it cast down its glorious rays. After weeks of relentless non-stop work, Mako felt he deserved a day of rest, so he carried young Zach down to the island's beach, where Izal joined them.

The sea was flat calm. Mako lay out on a smooth,

flat boulder, enjoying the warmth. With watchful eyes he looked on at the toddler crawling around in the sand at the water's edge, chasing after Izal who was playing with him.

The bird would stand still long enough for Zach to get near enough to touch him, but the second he would reach out to try, Izal would flutter his wings and fly a few yards away so the game would start all over again. No matter how many times this happened, little Zach would never cry or get upset; he would just laugh joyfully and keep on trying.

*Caw!*

Upon hearing his friend's call, Mako saw that his eyes were green.

*The boy is relentless.*

"I can see that."

*He shows no sign of tiring and never gets disheartened.*

"Two very good qualities for one tasked with the challenges that await a Watcher in the making."

*His speed is increasing,* Izal said, before moving over to another area as Zach was getting a little too close.

Mako sat up and continued to watch the little game. They played it every day as a sort of early training tactic. Zach was too young for any other type of training session. But this game, of Izal's devising, trained Zach's stamina, increased his speed, tested his determination, and pushed the limits of his energy. Zach was always improving.

"His speed is increasing, you're quite right," Mako said, voicing his observations. "There's still room for improvement though."

*True.* As he replied, Izal took his eyes away from Zach and looked to Mako, who met his gaze.

With Izal's concentration elsewhere, Zach used the following seconds to the best of his ability. He pushed himself up, standing on his own two feet, and ran with a speed that neither Mako or Izal knew he possessed. In the time it took to blink, Zach had closed the distance and leaped up onto Izal's back.

*Caw!*

Mako could not believe what he had just witnessed. This was the first time he had seen the boy run and jump.

Izal meanwhile was jumping around, flapping his wings as he gently tried to get Zach off his back. The boy ignored him and was laughing victoriously.

*Caw!* Izal called out. Seeing that nothing was working, his dark eyes turned green as they flashed at Mako.

*A little help here if you wouldn't mind!*

Mako chuckled and leaped to his aid. The way Izal was hopping about resembled a crazed interpretive dance.

Taking a gentle approach, Mako gingerly reached out and scooped up the young Zach, taking him up into his arms and carrying him over to another part of the beach.

"Come on, trouble, let's give Uncle Izal a rest."

A happy chuckle was the reply that the Guardian received.

*Thank you,* Izal said, and preened himself.

Mako put Zach down so he could crawl around some more. He joined Izal.

"I didn't know Zach could run."

*Neither did I,* Izal replied, feeling somewhat shocked. *But at least we know now.*

"True and it seems that on both feet he is much faster than either of us thought."

*And that he has passed the stage of walking and...* At that moment, Izal's train of thought was interrupted as he watched Zach stand up and start running directly toward them.

"Taking to running and jumping." Mako said, finishing Izal's thought just before Zach leaped up at Mako, who reacted instinctively caught him.

"Zach, what's wrong?" Mako asked, seeing worry

and fear on the boy's face.

"Shy, shy, sh..." Zach said, attempting to speak.

Man and raven both looked intently at him, awaiting his first word.

"Shanzi!" Zach whimpered.

*Caw!*

*His first word,* Izal said.

"And his first warning," Mako said, worry in his voice.

*Warning? How so?*

"It is no coincidence that his first word would be Shanzi. It is a warning and proof that I was right."

*Right about the Shanzi coming?*

"And now they are here, among us, and young Zach is no way near being ready for them." Mako's eyes hardened. "We are now on borrowed time. We need to step up his training, start everything even earlier than intended."

*As you wish.*

"Let's go. We've got work to do."

# CHAPTER VIII:

## *Fighting in the Forest*

**M**any a development had taken place on the Isle of Iris. Zach was now almost twelve years old and just over five feet tall. His blond hair was even brighter and more unruly than before, but the joyful smile remained.

His once perfect pale skin had taken on more color, and now bore the scratches and scars not only of a child, but of a Watcher in training.

His upper left arm bore a mark of the deepest black. It was not a tattoo, but had burned itself there soon after he spoke his first word. It was in the form of a perfect circle.

To one side of it was a crescent moon and seated in the heart of the circle, touching the top and four other areas within the circle, sat a five star pentacle, riding alongside the moon.

It was the Mark of the Shanzi, given to a Child of Tormenta, whenever there was a strong presence of the Dark Ones, in the world.

During the last five years, a war had started in a far off Realm, only to end after twenty-one months as the whole Realm fell under the control of the Shanzi. The Dark Ones now had their foothold on the world and were readying for their attacks on the other Realms.

The sky above Iris was cloudy, but the sun was able to filter through, bringing some light down onto the world. Standing in the forest, was none other than Zach himself. In his right hand he firmly gripped his thirty inch long wooden sword.

Zach's eyelids were shut and his ears were attuned to every noise that he heard. He stood perfectly still, holding his breath, his heart beating very, very slowly.

All around him, Zach could hear the snaps of twigs, the rustling of leaves, the calls and tweets of the local birds, and on his skin he could feel a soft, gentle breeze.

Just then he heard the noise he was listening out for, the sound of a spring, followed by a wooden target emerging from the trees. His eyes shot open as he ran toward the target before he leapt over it and unleashed a volley of strikes with his wooden sword, normally kept tied to his belt. One strike vertical, slicing down the spine of the target, whereas the others were both horizontal, each one hitting either side of the head.

*Caw!*

Zach turned to his right and saw Izal flying toward him; judging by the bird's speed, he figured he must be in some kind of trouble. Izal was now ten feet away and he showed no signs of stopping, he was coming straight for Zach.

*Caw!*

Moving as quickly as he could, Zach wasted no time in diving off to his right, he only just successfully dodged the raven, which went on to fly straight into the target.

*Smash!*

Now in pain, Izal showed no sign of slowing, instead choosing to soar, flying straight for Zach. Always light on his feet, Zach leaped up onto a tree, jumping from one branch onto another and onto another.

With Izal hot on his heels, Zach was moving to the best of his abilities, leaping and running along the longer branches, jumping only when he could run no more. His breathing fast, and his heart racing, pumping blood like there was no tomorrow.

Izal was still coming after him. Zach knew he had no other choice.

He knew he needed to gain some height, but first he

would need to lose some, so to trick Izal, he jumped forward only to grab hold of the thin branch he just left and swung himself back onto it, and then did a back flip off and landed on the lower branch of a shorter tree.

From his new position, Zach leaped to the closest tree and kicked himself toward another tree, giving him some of the needed height he required before suddenly, he side-flipped off the branch and fell. A well timed fall, which saw him land easily on Izal's back.

Now in control of the relentless bird, Zach forced him to fly back down to the ground. Izal wasn't enjoying having a passenger on this flight, especially a passenger who had taken control and was now piloting him like an aircraft.

Zach manoeuvred the raven to make it fly out of the forested area and steered him into a clearing where a large wooden cage waited for him.

In that moment Izal knew what Zach had planned, but it was too late. Zach leaped off at the last minute, leaving Izal to fly straight into the cage. With his prey inside, Zach kicked the door shut and locked it.

"That fast enough for you?" Zach asked in his youthful, confident voice, flashing a kind-hearted smile. The language that he spoke was the Mari dialect, taught to him by Mako.

*Caw!*

Confined, Izal struggled to break free and escape, but it was no good. The wood was too strong and refused to give.

"Don't struggle, you won't break this cage." Zach said.

*Caw!*

"Now, where is..." Zach stopped himself from finishing his own question, no longer needing to ask it. The answer came to him for he could sense and hear a presence behind him. Zach tightened his grip on his sword and slashed out at an arrow that shot out of the trees, breaking it in two.

"Hello, Mako," Zach greeted as he twirled the sword in his hand before slashing a second arrow.

*Caw!*

Zach looked to the cage; the raven's eyes were green, a tell-tale sign that the bird was up to something.

A third arrow fired at the cage, heading for the locking mechanism.

"Oh no, you don't!" Zach leaped toward the arrow and let loose with a kick, his timing perfect as he struck the arrow and shattered it.

*Caw!*

Izal flapped his wings and looked on at Zach, who stood proudly, wearing a happy grin.

"We can do this all day. How about coming out to face me?" Zach called out to the trees.

Mako stepped out into the clearing, bow and quiver in hand.

Zach looked at the weapon, recognizing the curves and the overall design. The bow was one that Zach himself had made upon his master's instruction.

"I see you're using my own bow against me." Zach couldn't help but look at his creation.

"You're right. Perhaps I should use one of your own swords instead." As Mako replied, he placed the bow down on the ground, drawing a wooden long sword from his belt. With a weapon in hand, Mako ran at his young student.

Zach sidestepped one swing, jumped over the second, and ducked under the third before he let out a few swings of his own, which Mako successfully countered.

"You'll have to do better than that!" Mako said.

"Fine!"

Upon his master's command, Zach unleashed a volley of swipes once more, unleashing slashes of all directions, but being the superior swordsman that Mako was, he was able to shield and defend himself masterfully.

"A real target is harder to hit, hey, Zach," Mako said.

"Ah! But you forget Master..." Zach leaped over Mako and kicked him in the back before swinging low with his sword, striking Mako's legs, sending him to the floor.

"...I'm faster than you."

Mako leaped up onto his feet and dusted himself off. "That's a good move, an appropriate use of a speed boost."

"I learned from the best." Zach said.

"I am glad that you remember what I had told you before, sword skills are very important, but against a more skilled or powerful opponent--"

"--sword skills aren't enough, fighting skills and good timing are just as important and are vital abilities to have." Zach finished his mentor's sentence.

"Very good, now remember, I don't want to see what you can do with a sword, I want to see what you can do."

"Right!"

Zach's grip tightened once again before he ran to his trainer, except instead of going for an attack, he jumped to the side and raced into the forest, hiding amongst the trees. He wasn't escaping or being a coward, but was actually trying out a tactic that would win him the battle.

# CHAPTER IX:

## *The Results Are In*

Inside the cage, Izal had nothing else to do but observe the events, watching Mako and Zach clash before Zach had darted off. The whole thing with him and Mako attacking Zach was part of an important training session. Ever since that day down on the beach, the Watcher's education had begun and now after all the years that passed, this important session had come, for it was the exam that would determine if Zach would advance to the next crucial stage.

"Come out, come out where ever you are!" Mako called, watching the trees for any sign of movement.

Just like he did minutes before with Izal, Zach hid in the forest, moving in between the trees, running along the branches and leaping from tree to tree before he leaped up into the sky, emerging from the forest, and landed behind Mako.

Zach delivered a hard double kick to Mako's spine, who instead of falling to the ground, remained standing and shook off the attack.

Continuing to act, Zach quickly back-flipped, only to then dive forward, flinging himself at his teacher, tackling him to the dirt before throwing a well-aimed kick at the wooden long sword, knocking it away. He thrust his own sword against Mako's throat.

"Was that what you wanted to see?" Zach asked.

"Yes, it was." Mako flashed a quick smile at Zach.

*Caw!*

Izal called out, just in case the two swordsmen had forgotten about him.

"Now that our session is done for today, how about

you let me up?"

Zach pulled his sword away and did as he was asked. He retrieved Mako's sword and passed it to him.

"I suppose I should let Easel out now?" Zach asked, saying the raven's name wrong.

"Izal," Mako said.

"Pardon?"

"It's Izal."

"What did I say?"

"Easel," Mako said.

"Oh, sorry." Zach said.

"Amazing. You can speak six languages fluently and yet, even now you still can't say a simple name," Mako said as he and Zach walked to the cage. "Do me a favor, say *eyes*," Mako said.

"Eyes," Zach repeated.

"Now say *all*."

"All."

"Now say both words together."

*"Eyes All."*

"Good, now say the two words a little faster."

"Izal," Zach said, finally getting the name right.

"There you go, you did it."

"Thank you, master." Zach bowed.

"Now if you remember that, you will never get our friend's name wrong again."

"Izal," Zach repeated as he walked over to the cage and opened it, letting the bird out. "I hope I didn't hurt you!" Zach said.

*You didn't,* Izal replied to the young lad, using the same type of telepathic link he had with Mako.

"What do you think of the cage?" Mako asked as he looked toward the wooden prison that Zach himself had constructed.

*It's very good, the door locked fine and the cage held. It refused to break and showed no weaknesses,* Izal said. *It's a fine piece of woodwork.*

"There you have it. Izal approves of your cage building skills. Now let us move onto the weapons." Mako checked out the wooden long sword for any damage, but there was none.

Zach and Izal looked on intrigued as the Iris Guardian examined the sword in detail.

"Let's see, there's an appropriate blade length of one meter. A well-crafted point..." Mako placed a finger on the pointed edge. "...no signs of damage sustained and it didn't break at any point during our little clash. It held out and took on your fierce, determined strikes with no problems." He nodded at his pupil. "As for the weight, it is spot on and supplies plenty of power and is quite the versatile weapon. Based on my observations, I can honestly say you have hand crafted a superb wooden sword, so well done."

Izal looked to Zach, who was happy with the review of the sword.

*Well done, kid,* the raven said.

"Now the bow--bring it to me, will you?" Mako asked.

Zach nodded and performed a quick bow before darting off to where Mako left it. Picking up the bow and quiver of arrows, he then ran over to older Watcher and handed them to him. "Here you are, Master."

"Thank you, Zach. Now let's see..." Mako said as he began to examine the bow. "...the shape of it is nothing less than perfect and the elasticity cannot be any better. It's nice and light with plenty of punch. This is a good bow and is worthy of putting in a shop to sell and sell it would. With my observation over, I can say that on your carpentry skills, you pass. After three years you have learned a lot, but there is more for you to learn."

"Yes, Master." Zach was happy. Ever since the age of five, woodwork had become a very important part of his learning.

"On carpentry you have proven yourself to start your learning of how to manufacture longbows, crossbows, and much more. As for your stamina and skill, you were clever enough to evade both Izal and myself by taking to the trees, displaying tactical cunning, where you used your speed and strength to move around the trees and overcome us. So on stamina and your own personal skill, you pass." Mako explained.

*Two for two, kid, not bad,* Izal said.

"As for written exams..."

*Here we go,* Izal said to Zach.

"...that you had taken this morning and all throughout this week..." Mako paused to look at Zach's anxious face. "...I can now reveal that you passed on all six language exams and you passed your exams on carpentry theory, history and navigational studies, as well. So that's another pass for you, well done. Now let's talk sword skills."

*Brace yourself, kid,* Izal said.

"You swing with no hesitation, you possess a perfect timing to defending yourself and when in your hand, it is like the sword becomes an extension of your own arm and you exercise perfect control. It is because of all the reasons I have just mentioned that I have no other choice but..." Mako grinned as he paused, creating a bit of tension. "...to pass you. Well done, Zach, you have passed all the factors and have earned the rank of a Watcher's Apprentice and are no more just a student."

*Well done, kid!* The raven congratulated.

"Thank you, Master Mako! Thank you, Master Izal!" Zach cried, overjoyed as he hugged both man and bird. He was most ecstatic about the fact that Mako approved of his sword skills.

From the moment he turned three, a wooden sword was placed in his hands. Since that day, he would spend twenty hours a week practicing and perfecting his swordsmanship.

"You have worked hard, Zach, I know I push you, but as you have proved this week, all your hard training has paid off."

"I know, Master," Zach bowed respectively to those who had been there for him every step of the way.

"Let's go to the house; you can have the rest of the day off."

"I appreciate that, I do, but I think I'll stay here for a bit longer, do a bit of practicing. Work on my archery for a bit," Zach said.

"You sure?" Mako asked.

"Yes, Master."

"In that case, you'll need these then." Mako passed his protégée the bow and the quiver.

"Thank you, Master." Zach said.

"Just don't overdo it and don't be too long. Izal and I will be up at the house preparing dinner."

"I'll see you later then," Zach said before he started to head toward the trees.

"Oh, before I forget," Mako called.

"Yeah?" Zach asked as he turned toward the man and the bird.

"I have a surprise for you up at the house."

"What kind of surprise?" Zach asked.

"You'll find out soon enough." Without another word, Mako grabbed hold of one of Izal's legs before the two of them flew off toward the house, leaving Zach to practice.

# CHAPTER X:

## *Mako's Lack of Faith*

Inside the house, Izal stood over by the fireplace, whereas Mako was closing the curtains, darkening the interior.

*So Zach passed,* Izal stated.

"Yes," Mako countered pleasantly as he walked over to the bird.

*You doubted whether he would pass, didn't you?* Izal asked, reading the doubt in Mako's head.

"Yes," he admitted.

*Why?*

"The theory I knew he would pass easily, the written work never poses a problem for students..."

*But?*

"I guess I doubted if he had the skill," Mako confessed.

*But why? You've spent the last eight years training him, just like you do with all your pupils.*

"I know, but normally when I put them through the exam, they are..."

*Twelve years old, so?*

"I just thought that Zach would be a little too young, that his age would impact his overall performance." Mako walked over to the dining table by the wall and sat down on a stool.

*But it didn't, he passed fine,* Izal retorted,–flying over to Mako.

"Exactly, he did fine. His results matched those of students who had the same length of training as him and that's the problem."

*How so?*

"Zach's training has been more intense than that of my former students and unlike them, he is a Child of Tormenta. Compared to the rest of my pupils, he should be far more superior, more advanced, but he's not, he's just equal." Mako sighed and shrugged his shoulders.

*I see. You believe Zach isn't anywhere near his true potential, but tell me, are you really comparing him to your former students or are you comparing him to you?*

Mako looked sourly at Izal. He couldn't believe his feathered friend would think something like that, let alone to utter those words to him.

"What is that supposed to mean?" Mako asked testily.

*You yourself are a Child of Tormenta, an exemplary one at that.*

"So what?"

*As a child you were truly gifted.*

"And?"

*Zach isn't you. He is his own person, so you shouldn't compare him to you or to any of your previous students,* Izal replied, defending Zach.

"I'm not, but he has been taught by the both of us and has been trained harder than any of my former students, harder than myself." A fire was starting to burn in Mako's eyes. "Even with all that extra training, Zach is only equal."

*Yes. Equal to your best students though,* Izal replied.

"But he should be better!" Mako shouted. "The Shanzi are here, they have claimed the Indiania realm and are now mounting their attack on others. It will not be long before they reach Mares."

*I know all of this!*

"The Shanzi are stronger this time, they're different!"

*How so?*

"The Guardian of Indiania, just before he died, he

reported a difference in them. He said they were much stronger, faster, smarter, and have newer forms. This time we are faced with a new breed of Shanzi. The Shanzi have..."

*Evolved.* Izal said, interrupting Mako.

"Exactly. Not only are they back, they've improved themselves. Zach will never stand a chance against them. I taught the Guardian of Indiania and he only lasted five minutes and he was a Great Guardian."

Mako's words hit Izal hard.

*Well maybe, just maybe, the reason why Zach is not as good as he should be is because of you!* Izal's mind roared defensively.

"What is that supposed to mean?"

*Two decades, twenty years have passed since your last student, until Zach arrived. He's been your only student in the last thirty-one years. Maybe given the years that went by, you've lost your knack.*

"Just exactly what are you saying?"

*I'm saying maybe you're not as good as an instructor as you used to be.*

"How dare you!" Mako replied, enraged.

*I'm sorry, Mako. I was out of line.*

"Yes, you were, but Zach is not ready or anywhere near being ready. He's still using a wooden sword, for crying out loud!"

*So?*

"It has been seven years and he is still using wood. He's almost twelve now..."

*Yes, almost twelve, the age all your students are when they receive a real sword,* Izal replied as nicely as he could.

"That's true, but unlike Zach, they started using wood at the age of five. In this aspect, Zach is behind, sure he started learning with a sword sooner, but he has spent more time using wood than any of my other students."

Izal had no other choice but to agree. Mako was quite right. Zach was the only student out of many to still be using a wooden weapon.

Normally when it came to the education of warriors, the actual lessons and training started at the age of five and continued till the age of sixteen. Students who proved to be slower were still in training until they turned eighteen. Some were still students in their twenties.

*The only thing that stopped you from giving Zach a proper sword was you!*

"It doesn't matter now! None of this matters, not anymore!" Mako barked as he got up and kicked his stool. "Zach is not ready and he never will be! The Shanzi are going to destroy everything."

*How dare you say such a thing?* In that moment, Izal glared at Mako, flapping his wings angrily.

"It is the truth. Izal, Zach will be a Good Guardian, but he will never be a Great Watcher and a Good Guardian is not and never will be a match for the Shanzi. This time the Dark Ones will win."

# CHAPTER XI:

## *The Midnight Kiss*

The sun was gone, the sky dark and young Zach was lurking outside Mako's house, leaning against the wooden paneling, standing between the window on the western side and the front door. With his head turned inward to the window, he was listening in to the heated conversation inside the house.

For the last thirty minutes Zach had spent the time concealing his thoughts, listening in, hearing all of Mako's spoken words and having Izal's thoughts pass through his head.

A single tear ran down his face when he heard Mako's lack of faith in him, deeply saddening him. He couldn't believe it; all he ever did was try his best and from what he was hearing, his best just isn't good enough.

Zach couldn't bear to hear another word, so he gently removed his hand from the door handle and began walking away. Taking great care not to make a single sound, he couldn't help but let a few more tears run down his youthful face and let his feelings scream, feelings of betrayal, uselessness and anger.

All throughout the conversation Izal had defended him, but Mako, the man Zach respected, admired, idolized, and loved, had done nothing but put him down and insult him. Zach so wanted to let out his thoughts, let them develop, run around his head, even voice them, but he couldn't, not yet.

Izal's ability of telepathy not only projected his thoughts into the minds of others, but he could also link with them, connecting their minds, granting him access to their every thought.

Given Zach's close proximity, Izal would be able to hear his every thought, but Izal isn't the only one on the Isle of Iris to possess such a skill.

Children of Tormenta were often gifted with a special ability or two and Zach, like the other children, also possessed an ability. Like Izal, he was telepathic. Neither had told Mako yet. Izal was waiting to see how his skills developed.

From the day Izal learned that he and Zach shared the same power, he took him under his wing and engaged in a new type of training, teaching him how to master his telepathy ability and improve it greatly. With the raven's help, Zach had learned to establish mind links and extend it so that he was able to sense the presence of all living life forms.

Zach had developed his abilities so well that he could now distinguish the difference in life signals, enabling him to tell species apart. He could even tell how strong they are by reading the strength of their life-force, and had learned to read auras that would indicate if a being has good or bad intentions.

Izal had also taught Zach how to mask his own life force, enabling him to make his presence vanish without a trace, resulting in him being unable to be traced. Due to his excessive practice at perfecting his gifts, Zach had become a pro at hiding his life force and was forever using it against Izal.

The young Watcher now stood at the edge of the volcano, next to the trees that Mako used for his Flight of Iris. Here stood a wooden post with a long line anchored on it. The line ran all the way down to the Nogmal forest. For Zach, it was a zip-line.

Removing his black leather belt from his waist, with his wooden sword still attached, he threw one end over the line, and caught it, holding an end in each hand.

Leaping forward and away from the edge of the

volcano, Zach started to slide downward, speeding down and putting as much distance between him and Mako, as he possibly could.

*So I'm not ready! I'm not special enough! Not exemplary!* Zach thought to himself, feeling safe to let loose his thoughts.

Working his way down the line, Zach gazed upward at the night sky. A crescent moon shone brightly, sending down its silvery rays.

Thousands of tiny stars were dotted across the vast field of darkness. Even with anger in his heart, Zach couldn't help but smile at such a beautiful sight.

*I'm not the one who failed, Mako-- you did!* Zach let go of the belt, pulling it away from the line. Nowhere near the end of the line, he began to fall.

Zach could feel his heart beating erratically as he plummeted down to the earth below him, knowing he was only seconds away from instant death and he showed no fear.

"Die..." he said, as he closed his eyes and felt his heart begin to slow "...or live?" Finishing off his question, his eyes shot open and his heart stopped completely.

His heart was not the only thing to freeze. In that moment everything froze. Zach lay frozen in mid-air three meters above a Nogmal tree that was ready to impale him. In the space of a second, everything had begun to move again.

Rolling to his right, Zach spun his body 270° degrees to dodge a thick branch. In his perspective of the immediate situation, everything seemed to be slowed down, the seconds lasting as long as minutes, giving him more than enough time to manoeuvre his way around. In truth, Zach was moving faster than a flash of lightning.

When dangerously close to impact with the ground, he threw forth his belt around a strong thin branch and grabbed the other end with his free hand before pulling tightly. Using all the gathered force from his fall to propel himself upward, he swung himself sideways, side flipping to his left, landing safely on a branch.

Keeping his momentum going, he back-flipped off onto a much lower branch and then dived off that, only to land on the earth below. With solid ground beneath him and his fall over, Zach put his belt back on and straightened his sword.

"You say I am nowhere near ready and yet I can let go off a zip-line and free-fall at a dangerous speed and yet still land safely. Tell me, could any of your former students do that?" Zach called out into the night, his question aimed at his master.

Even in near darkness, Zach noticed three wooden posts and five man-shaped targets, so he pulled free his sword and twirled it in his hands, eager to engage in a little training.

"I'll show you!" Zach snarled through clenched teeth.

Running forward in the moonlit area, he charged at the target that was closest and jumped up, giving himself some height as he lashed out with a kick, his right leg shooting out and striking the wooden man in his chest. Upon landing, he let out a quick slash, delivered with such force that it decapitated the target, sending the wooden head flying into the trees, exploding upon impact.

Moving on, Zach advanced onto a target and unleashed a short volley of swings to loosen up his arms before he leaped over to two wooden men positioned a few meters apart. He lashed out at the target to his left, taking off its left arm before striking the one to his right.

In the seconds that followed, he coordinated his attacks between the two men, two slashes at one and then two at the other and with every swing of his sword came a little flip or a jump.

He kept up his constant display of swordplay until

nothing remained of the two targets except for two piles of broken wood.

With two more wooden men down, Zach turned his attention to the fourth man and charged it. Running at full speed, he tackled the man to the ground, plunging his sword into the chest area. Given the sheer force of his attack, part of the chest broke, as did most of his sword, shattering to almost nothing.

"Useless!" Zach grunted in frustration, throwing the handle of his ruined weapon off to one side.

Just because he was now unarmed, Zach wasn't going to let that fairly substantial fact prevent him from destroying the fifth wooden man.

Acting the only way he knew how—quickly—Zach pushed his feet hard against the ground, propelling himself skyward before he would come crashing back down to earth, but this was his intention.

He was going to land directly on top of the last tree man, so he prepared a little something for the target. With all his might, he slammed his hardened elbow into the head of the man, shattering it, sending splinters and shards everywhere.

Back on his feet, Zach didn't hesitate to attack again, so he threw a right handed open palm punch to the chest, which was followed by a harsh left handed double jab and then he spun round on the spot, delivering a powerful roundhouse kick to the right arm, but he didn't stop there either. Zach had one more attack planned before he would be finished with this target. It is now time for him to use the move he called the Midnight Kiss.

Zach pulled his right arm back, his hand open and perfectly flat as it rested against his hip, his open palm facing outward, while his left arm was across his body and his left hand open like his right hand, but facing the opposite way. His left hand sitting on top of his right, wrist on wrist.

He pushed out with his right hand as he slid his left arm away from his body, turning his hand round as he aligned it with his right before throwing both arms outward, fully extending them, and striking the target squarely in the chest. Zach delivered the attack with so much speed and strength that the target exploded.

Zach dropped to his knees, his hands all scratched, bleeding, and hurting like hell, as did his elbow. He was in such pain that he could no longer ignore it and his breathing was hard and he wanted to cry. Just as he was about to allow himself to shed another tear, he suddenly sensed something.

He raised his head, scanning the trees and ignoring the pain coursing throughout his body. Whoever it is, the presence is strong and powerful.

"Who's there?" Zach called out, jumping to his feet.

"Someone who is very, very impressed by you!" a raspy masculine voice replied, catching Zach off guard.

# CHAPTER XII:

## *Stranger of the Night*

"Who said that?" Zach tried to hide the fear in his voice, but he just couldn't do it. After all, just because he was a warrior in training, he was still an unarmed eleven-year-old boy, out in a forest, in the middle of the night, with an unknown entity nearby. Zach had every reason to be afraid.

"You fear me, how intriguing," the raspy voice commented, its deathly tones drifting through the trees.

"Who's there?" Zach called out, clenching his fists as he tried to find out where the voice was coming from, but his eyes failed him.

Zach's fear was growing as he was unable to spot the owner of the ghostly voice who refused to answer his questions, leaving him no other choice but to use his sensing abilities.

"I will find you!" Zach yelled as he closed his eyes and began to search everything.

Everywhere he scanned he could read a huge power level, a life-force with so much energy that it radiated throughout the surrounding trees. At first Zach thought that this power was all over but he quickly realized that he was being naïve. The power he could feel was coming from a sole entity, an entity that was moving so fast that it felt like it was everywhere, but the thing that Zach couldn't do was read the aura of the unseen being, preventing him from being able to tell if the entity is good or bad.

Suddenly the powerful life force disappeared, vanishing completely, but Zach knew in his heart that the unidentified creature was still in the area. This was confirmed when Zach was unable to feel the gentle breeze that only seconds ago, was blowing against his back.

"Found you!" Zach said silently, his lips barely moving.

Everything was still and Zach could feel something directly behind him. He could feel it due to his highly-tuned sensory skill, but the presence behind him felt weaker, giving off a lower energy reading, which told Zach one thing. The being was able to lower his power. Without another thought Zach leaped skyward and tosses himself backward in mid-air, allowing him to flip over the tall man behind him.

"Now I'm behind you!"

"Ha, ha, ha, ha!" The tall man laughed, unnerving Zach. "Your speed is impressive for a boy of your age."

"Who are you?" Zach asked.

The man still had his back to him. All Zach could see was the man's long, thick, disheveled hair. Hair darker than night itself, fell to his waist.

"I am someone who is very impressed by your skills," the man replied, turning to face Zach, letting him see him for the first time.

He was six-foot two-inches tall, taller than Mako, and very thin. He wore a black monk's robe, tied closed with a narrow black rope. On his feet, he wore jet-black boots. All of his exposed skin was ghostly pale, with a grayish tinge. His nose was small and flat, with narrow slits for nostrils; his mouth wide, exposing razor-sharp teeth. He had long bony fingers with two-inch long black nails, resembling claws.

But it was his eyes that held Zach's attention. They were wide and angled, white as moons save for the very small, very dark pupils, eyes of pure darkness. His dark eyebrows mingled with his hair.

Looking up at the hellish looking face, Zach at first felt fearful, but then realized that he could feel no evil coming from this man. He let go of his fear and instead was filled with curiosity.

"Who are you?" This time Zach asked more confidently.

"I am Shimay and you are Zach," the man answered. His voice was raspy and travelled on the wind.

"H-h-how do you know my name?" Zach stuttered as he took four steps back from Shimay.

"Oh I know a lot about you, I have watched over you from the day you arrived here." Shimay confessed.

Zach was unsure whether to speak or not.

"I have been with you all these years."

"You couldn't have done, I would have seen you!" Zach stammered.

"No, you wouldn't," the man replied, grinning broadly. "You're only seeing me now because I'm letting you."

"What?"

"Unlike you, Mako and Izal, I am not among the living." Shimay's eyes widened as he spoke.

"Then what are you?"

"I'm what you'd call a phantom. Something that died long ago, but even in death I am trapped, unable to leave."

"Leave what?" Zach asked.

"Leave this island, of course. This is where I died, but I did not meet my end, so I live on in spirit." As he spoke, Shimay took a step closer to Zach.

"Why were you here when you died?"

"I used to live here. I was the Iris Guardian before I was brutally murdered by a student of mine."

"Why?"

"He wanted my title, I guess, to take over my position and begin a new life teaching the future generation of Watchers. I could not rest so I rose from my grave and have lived in secret ever since, living among the trees, watching the future Watchers. Mako is the Guardian of Iris and I am the Spirit of Iris," the phantom divulged.

"So why reveal yourself to me?" Zach had a very odd feeling about the current situation.

"Because you are special, Zach. I can see how strong and fast you really are. No force, good or bad, stands a chance against you."

"Mako doesn't seem to think so," Zach muttered bitterly.

"That is because that old fool can only see what you can do, but me, I can see into your soul and see just how strong you are. There is so much power and speed that you're not using, but you've locked it away, burying it completely."

"You really believe that?"

"Do I believe that you are not currently using your true power? No. And do you know why?"

"Why?"

"Because I don't need to *believe* it to be true. I *know* it is true."

Shimay's words brought a smile to Zach's face.

"And more importantly, I can help you unlock it!" Shimay declared.

Zach was speechless, both thrilled and awed. He couldn't help but think that the night was getting stranger and stranger with each passing second.

"You can really help me?" Zach asked.

"Yes, Zach, I can help you," Shimay boasted. "I can train you and I can make you greater than you already are and greater than Mako himself."

"But why?"

"Mako is your master and yet he is failing you, doubting you, but I do not. You are the future, Zach, and I have every faith in you. As a past guardian and a former mentor, I cannot stand by and watch you not achieve your full potential." Shimay's words sat well with Zach, but a small bit of doubt remained.

"Why should I trust you? I don't know you."

"Because I took a vow, a vow I will uphold even in death."

"Answer me this, if you really are a former Guardian, then why do you look so demonic?"

Zach's question did not surprise Shimay. "Because death is not pretty and I was a victim of murder. It was an ugly act and it left me looking as I do."

"I'm still not sure."

"I understand. I wouldn't want to pressure you into doing something you didn't want to, but ask yourself, who would you rather learn from? A washed-up old man with no faith in you, or me, a phantom that could make you the most memorable Watcher in all of existence? The choice is yours." Shimay's voice was calm and controlled and yet contained a hint of menace.

"You can make me greater than Mako?" Out of nowhere came a craving for power that filled Zach's whole being.

"Yes, I can, and I can teach you so much!" Shimay knew in his cold dead heart that Zach was now his.

"What's the catch?"

"There is no catch, just two rules that you'll have to obey, if I am to be your mentor."

"What rules?" Zach stepped nearer.

"Rule one is from this point on you will trust me completely, following my every command and instruction."

"And your second rule?"

"You tell no one of my existence, not Mako or Izal."

"But..."

"But, but nothing. For centuries I have lived on this island in secret. No one can know of my existence."

"I'm not sure." Zach felt really uneasy; he didn't feel right about keeping a secret of this magnitude from his two father figures, but he desired to learn the power that Shimay was offering to teach him.

"Understandable. You have cause for your hesitation, but before you write me off, how about a quick demonstration?"

"A demonstration?"

"Just watch!" Shimay instructed before he shimmered away, fading away into the night only to reappear in another spot among the trees before fading away again and appearing in another spot.

Shimay's disappearing act lasted for a full minute, a minute Zach spent feeling out Shimay's energy and watching the trees, his eyes dancing around his surroundings.

"But how, how is that--?" Zach stammered in awe as Shimay reappeared behind him.

"Possible?" Shimay interrupted, startling Zach. Zach turned and looked at him. "You can teleport!"

"No, but I can fly and I am very fast. With my help, you can be fast too."

"I'll do it! I accept your rules!" Zach declared, eager to become the spirit's apprentice.

"Good, now swear on it!" Shimay's eyes gleamed with delight.

"I swear, Master." Zach bowed out of respect.

*I have you now,* Shimay thought to himself, smiling.

"So when do we start training?" Zach's desire, his craving for power, was growing more and more.

"Right now. I hope you're not tired; we will be training all night."

"All night?"

"*All* night." Shimay said. "Now due to your lack of a true weapon, for now, enhancing your sword skills will have to wait, so until then we will work on speed and improve your already impressive fighting skills. So tell me, Zach, are you ready? Ready to unlock your potential?"

"I'm ready!" Zach replied with no hesitation.

"Then we'll begin."

.

# CHAPTER XIII:

## *Izal's Revelation*

It was a new day on Iris. Instead of being outside enjoying the glorious weather, Mako was inside his house, eating breakfast.

Although his face showed no sign of fear or worry, inside his mind was a different story. In the two hours he had been awake, he had made his bed, took an outside wash and had a quick training session. Then he voyaged back into the house, heading upstairs to Zach's room.

The room was a typical dorm room, with beds lined up either side. There was a single window covered by a violet curtain at one end of the room, opposite the door. On the opposite side of the room, Zach slept. His arming sword was mounted on the wall along with a certificate and various training swords. Here he found the bed already made, which was odd because Zach always made his bed after he'd eaten. Mako could only assume that the bed was not slept in and that Zach had not returned to the house. He went outside and searched, but found nothing. After that, he was hungry again, and fixed some buttered bread for himself and Zach.

Nearly finished with his meal, Mako looked at the plate next to his own, puzzling over Zach's failure to emerge. "How peculiar," Mako commented out loud.
As he thought about it, Mako realized he hadn't seen Izal either, not since the night before when they had their loud disagreement. Izal had flown off, not wanting to be in the same room as Mako, any longer. "Where are they?" Mako asked himself.

The aged swordsman finished his bread and then walked outside. He knew for certain that Izal was avoiding him, but as for Zach, Mako figured him to be out training, getting some morning practice, or slacking off somewhere. Trying to put it out of his mind, he decided that maybe a day of solitude and training would be good for him.

Two hours passed and Mako was still hard at it, plunging steel into wood as he struck his forged sword into the many targets now positioned around his home. Out of all his weapons, the black handled long sword was Mako's personal favorite.

The sword was doubled-edged, serrated on one side and straight-edged on the other. The hilt had emeralds embedded in it. Where the blade met the hilt, it bore the sign of the Watchers, a white eye with three triangles around it. Like all of Mako's weapons, it was kept lethally sharp and the two-handed weapon was exquisite in its versatility.

Mako thrust the weapon once again, the blade piercing straight through the wooden log. He chose to leave his sword in the target, noticing a large black bird flying above the Nogmal forest.

"Izal! Come to me!" Mako called out, hands cupped around his mouth.

*Caw!*

"Izal!" he called again, more insistently.

*No!* Izal boomed, his single word resounding loudly inside Mako's head.

"Izal, come!" Mako ordered.

*Fine!*

The raven flew higher, and then hurtled down at Mako in a show of speed and anger. Mako decided to ignore him and went to recover his sword and sheath it. When he turned around, Izal was glaring at him with brilliant green eyes.

*What?* Izal demanded.

"Izal, it's good to see you."

*What do you want?* Izal's telepathic tone was full of fury. *You haven't called me here to apologize, so what exactly do you want?*

"Apologize? I have nothing to apologize for!" Mako snapped, before turning away.

*Yes you do. Why have you summoned me here?* Izal replied, flicking his wings.

"Zach's not here and I haven't seen him all morning. In fact, I believe he didn't even come home last night."

*That's because he didn't. He spent all night in the forest.*

"Explain," Mako ordered, turning back round to face the bird.

*I could feel his energy coming from the forest; by the way it felt, I'd say he was training, but before I was able to find him I lost him.*

"What do you mean, you lost him? Your ability allows you to feel every life force within a two-mile radius. How could you lose him?" Mako asked harshly.

*What does it matter anyway? You have no faith in him!*

"How did you lose him?" Mako barked, ignoring Izal's remark.

*Foolish Mako, you write Zach off all because you still believe in that what you see is what you get. If you possessed even a fraction of my power, then you would be able to see what Zach is really capable off, able to see the power he has locked away.*

"What?" Mako asked, surprised.

*Ha! That boy, he possesses a strength equal to your own.*

"Don't make me laugh!" Mako said, interrupting Izal.

*And if trained right, it won't be long until his skills are greater than yours. I can see it clear as day when I look into his eyes and I have known this since the day he arrived here.* Izal said, finishing his thought.

"Then why didn't you tell me?"

*Because it is not my place to say. My job is to watch out for children and act as a messenger. Your job is to educate them,* Izal snapped.

"Don't lecture me! From day one you knew how important it is to get him ready and you withheld valuable information from me."

*Don't blame this on me! You're the one who failed to see his potential and help him achieve it.*

"Well, I know now. Now I can really push him in his education."

*It doesn't matter. You're too late!* Izal snapped.

"What do you mean by that?"

*What I mean is that Zach never came home last night and I can think of one good reason as to why that would be.*

"He was outside and overheard us!" Mako deduced.

*Yes.*

"How? You would have felt him."

*Not necessarily,* Izal replied.

Before Mako could say another word, Izal flapped his wings and flew on top of the pierced log.

"You didn't feel him last night and then you lost him a few hours later, how can that be? Is your power slipping?"

*My power is as good as ever, but Zach, he is getting very good with his power. Perhaps too good.*

"What power? Zach has no power!" Mako says disbelievingly.

*That's where you're wrong! Zach is like me; he possesses the ability of telepathy, mind-linking and he has extra sensory perception.* Izal knew he was betraying Zach's trust by exposing his secret, but it was the right thing to do.

"How did I not know? I should have been aware of this."

*You didn't know because he hid it well.*

75

"For how long?"

*A little over four years.*

"Four years!" Mako stammered.

*Yes.*

"You knew about this, and like Zach, you have kept it hidden from me for four years."

*Caw!*

"And what have you been doing in all that time?"

*Helping him.*

"Helping him?"

*Yes.*

"Helping him how?" Mako questioned as he gazed intently at the bird, which turned away.

*I've been helping him to develop his ability,* Izal boasted proudly. *But it seems I have taught him too well. I taught him how to mask himself and it seems he has learned to improve his capability and is now able to hide himself even from me.*

"And why would you teach him that particular skill?"

*You know as well as I do that Zach and I are not the only beings in existence to possess our particular skill. Many other beings have been known to have it, including the Shanzi. I taught him so he could use it to shield himself from enemies.* Izal confessed.

"Yes, and now he is using it against you. I guess I'm not the only one that Zach is avoiding."

Izal says nothing.

"I need to find him, talk to him."

*He won't listen to you.*

"I have to try," Mako said, walking to the house.

*In that case, I would try the forest.*

"The forest?" Mako asked.

*Until sunrise I kept detecting a power level there. It's your best bet.*

"Thank you, Izal," Mako said, most sincerely.

*You'll need more than words!* Izal called out.

"I have just the thing, something that I should have given him a lot sooner," Mako replied, pushing the door open and going inside.

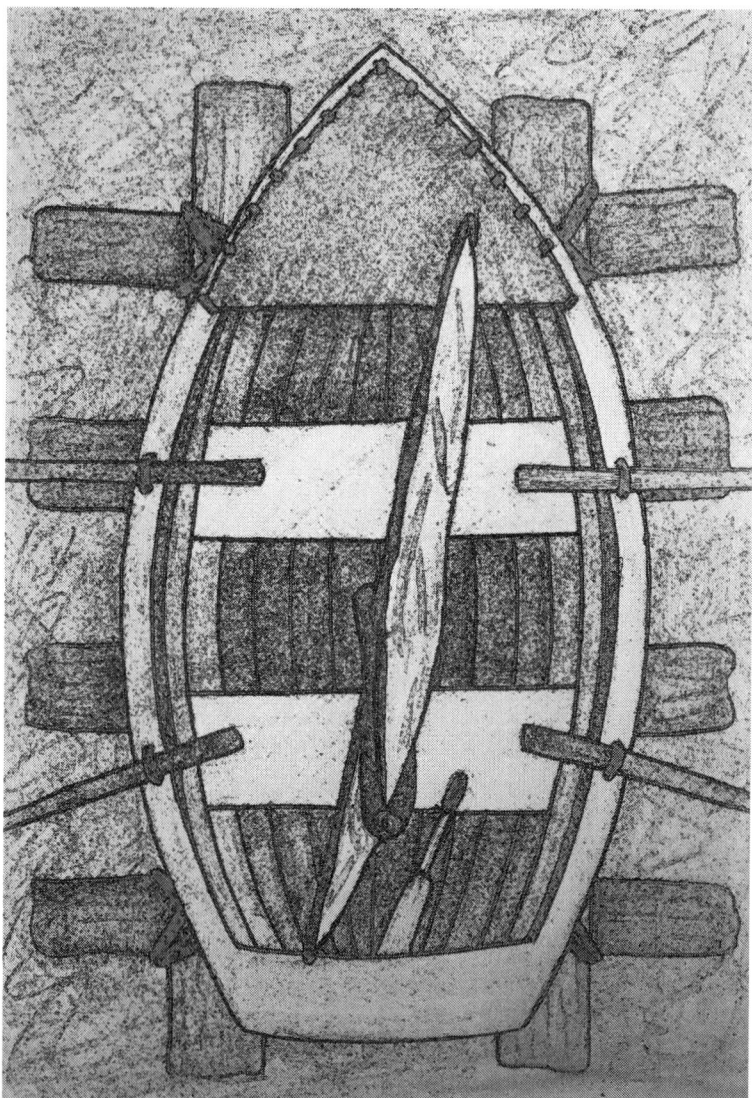

# CHAPTER XIV:

## *Down at Dead Man's Beach*

Zach was not in the forest, but was down at the beach, standing chest high in the water. He didn't bother with removing his clothes, preferring to keep them on. He wanted to have the added weight and drag that his clothes would create for him. The drag would slow him down whilst swimming and the extra weight would pull him down, making him sink. By swimming in these conditions, he was able to improve his swimming stamina and his strength.

His breathing was now nice and slow, fully controlled when only minutes ago it was hard and shallow. He couldn't help but think of how he spent his morning.

Every muscle in his body hurt, aching from the night's strenuous activities. From the moment he started training with Shimay, he spent the rest of the darkened hours practicing with no breaks, just endless hours of training. The only break came when the sun began to rise and Shimay chose to end their session, instructing Zach to leave the forest and get some rest before their next workout.

Preferring to avoid Mako and Izal, instead of going home, Zach headed to the beach, where he entered a cave. Here he found Mako's Delfini, a type of wooden rowboat, fitted with a mast and a set of sails. These boats were widely used all over the Mares realm.

The boat was three meters long and two meters wide at its widest point. It had a flat back and the usual pointed bow with a "U" shaped hull. It sat four people comfortably, two on each of the wooden benches that were on either side of the mast, which stood up from the centre of the boat. The mast has a noticeable bend to it, which at a distance looked like the top half of a bow, cut in half. It is because of its unique mast design that the Delfini got its name, for when the sails were deployed, from a distance the mast and sails looked just like a dolphin's dorsal fin.

The boat's rudder was also positioned in the centre of the boat between the two benches. This allowed anyone sailing the boat to have control of it.

The boat also has four small holes, two on either side of the boat by the benches to house the long oars. First and foremost, the Delfini was a row boat and the sails were used only to take advantage of the winds.

He looked inside the boat. Provided he lay underneath the seats, it was more than big enough for him to sleep in. He could have chosen to sleep on one of the twenty centimeter wide bench seats, which were also more than long enough for him to sleep on. However, being a restless sleeper, he chose to sleep on the floor rather than risk falling off a bench. He climbed aboard and crawled under the seats before finally passing out, only to wake two hours later.

Instead of opening his eyes and rising gently, Zach, in his semi-alert state had completely forgotten where he was. He sat up quickly and hit his head on the underside of one of the Nogmal seats, smacking the back of his head when he fell back down to the floor of the boat.

"Ow!" He winced, rubbing his forehead. "Note to self, don't do that again."

Zach crawled out from beneath the benches and climbed out of the boat. He left the cave, walking out into the brilliant sunlight, only to become temporally blinded by how bright the sun was. When his eyes adjusted and his vision returned, he walked over to the ocean's edge and looked at the calm, warm, inviting water.

Even though he had gone without dinner and was yet to have some breakfast, Zach didn't feel hungry at all.

He didn't even feel tired; the two hours of sleep were more than enough time to fully replenish his energy although he was still feeling the roaring pain in all his muscles.

"I guess I overdid it a bit," he said. "Maybe a couple of hours in the water will do me some good. It'll give my body some support anyway."

Upon his latest conclusion, Zach ran into the water and dived under when it was deeper than a meter. Beneath the surface, Zach held his breath as he swam his way through the underwater environment. He pushed himself for as long as he possibly could; eighty-six seconds.

"Surprisingly that doesn't feel too bad," Zach remarked, noting his lack of pain when immersed. "In that case, maybe I should do a lap."

By lap, Zach meant to swim round the whole of the Isle of Iris, and with no one around to tell him no, he got under way. Time passed quickly, and by the time he was done all of his muscles were screaming again. He swam over to where he could stand up and had a little rest, slowing his breathing back to normal and thinking about the training of the previous night.

To start with, Shimay had trained Zach like Izal had trained him back when he was a toddler, when Izal would land somewhere and Zach would have to try and catch him, only to have Izal fly off to another spot whenever Zach had got too close. The only difference was that Shimay's version was a lot faster and harder.

With his superior speed, Shimay was able to move all over the forest, easily dodging Zach. He had to chase Shimay down; moving as fast as he possibly could to even reach the spirit. Zach's knowledge of the trees allowed him to get close enough to Shimay to reach out and grab him, but the moment that Zach went to reach out, Shimay would vanish only to come into sight on a tree far off in the distance.

With overwhelming fatigue setting in, Zach put the

Blood Rush technique into effect. The method allowed Watchers to make their hearts beat at twice their normal speed, releasing fresh blood and a wave of adrenaline, fuelling the Watcher with new energy that allows them to move even faster than before. Zach had used this technique when he fell through the sky and manoeuvred his way around the trees.

With the Blood Rush aiding him, Zach's speed dramatically improved and he was now able to reach Shimay in half the time. Still, even with his greater speed, he still couldn't lay a finger on Shimay.

The length of any Blood Rush depended on a number of factors;–how physically drained a Watcher was and the amount of practice they had with it. The Blood Rush was quite powerful when being used in an act of desperation, a situation when the user was in trouble and needed the extra boost of energy. When used in such an act, the Blood Rush was more than enough to fully revive the user and normally lasted up to thirty seconds or so, depending on the person's own skill, greatly increasing their stamina and strength. When it had run its course, the user lost half the energy they had received, but they were able to carry on.

If not used in an act of desperation and when the user was fully energized, then the Blood Rush could last between five and forty minutes, extending their full power by a quarter. When the Blood Rush was spent, it left the user heavily drained, almost to the point of collapse. Even so, some Watchers had mastered the technique so well that they could maintain a Blood Rush for up to two hours.

Knowing the skill as well as he did, Zach knew the ability was better off being used when it was really required. Due to his failure to catch Shimay, even with his Blood Rush, Zach kept on using it, again and again, abusing it as one rush ended only to unleash another one. Zach was truly testing himself, as he pushed himself to his limit and beyond it.

After hours of effort, Zach was still unable to catch the spirit, but he was improving, getting faster and faster with every attempt. Noting his success, Shimay decided to change tactics and start training Zach in another way, one that would test Zach's defending capabilities.

Shimay had Zach stand in the middle of a nearby clearing and told him to close his eyes, and that no matter what Zach should keep them closed. Zach felt Shimay move away before his life force faded away, only to reappear in another spot. From its new position, Zach felt the spirit come flying at him and was knocked violently to the ground. He opened his eyes to see what happened.

"I told you to keep your eyes closed!" the spirit screamed as he flew away.

Zach quickly shut his eyes as he stood up, only to feel Shimay's power again just before he got hit in the face. This had gone on for another half an hour; thirty minutes of Zach sensing Shimay, but failing to move quickly enough to defend himself against the spirit's volley of attacks.

Now quite badly beaten, Zach knew he needed more power, more speed, so he used the Blood Rush once again. This time, due to being used in an act of desperation, it fully revived him, ending his pain and actually healing him of the open wounds he sustained from his beating.

But it could not conceal him. Every time he used the Blood Rush, his life force spiked and he was unable to mask it. As a result, anyone or anything capable of sensing his energy could find him easily. It also heightened his extrasensory capabilities, making it easier for him to find Shimay, seeing him in his mind. He was able to fend off every one of Shimay's attacks.

No matter how hard or fast he tried, he just couldn't land a hand on Zach. Not even when he upped his speed and tried masking his own power, Zach could still feel him and ward off his attacks.

Shimay kept his efforts up for a whole hour and in that hour he couldn't touch Zach once. Not only that, Zach only used his Blood Rush once. Due to his intense focus on defending himself from the constant attacks, he was able to maintain the technique for a full sixty minutes.

Training had ended shortly after the hour was over. Shimay needed to rest, as did Zach who couldn't help but notice how much his power had grown in one night. He was stronger, faster, had advanced his extrasensory abilities and brought his Blood Rush to a whole new level.

Suddenly the presence of a life force awakened Zach from his thoughts. Izal was coming.

*Time to go!*

# CHAPTER XV:

## *Back to the Forest*

Zach wasted no time, retreating inside the boat cave, his soaked clothes clinging to his body. Then he turned to look out, and realized he'd left tracks everywhere, on the sand and the rocks.

"Damn!" he exclaimed.

Zach closed his eyes and gave in to his power. In his mind's eye he could see Izal flying above the beach, scanning the shore for a clue to his whereabouts. He pushed a little harder, and gained entry into the bird's mind.

*Come on, Zach, where are you?* Izal asked.

Just then Zach's eyes opened and his vision of Izal was gone. He was pleased that Izal could no longer detect him by their shared link if he chose not to reveal himself.

"I'm just getting better and better!" Zach exclaimed. He closed his eyes and entered Izal's mind once more.

*Caw!*

*What do we have here? Ah, a couple of wet footprints.* Izal flew over to the tracks and began to inspect them.

*These are recent. I know you're here, Zach!*

*Damn it!*

*The prints lead to the boat cave. You're in there, aren't you, Zach?*

In his mind, Zach could see the raven closing in on his hiding spot.

*He's going to find me, unless...* Zach cut off his own thought as an idea came to him.

*I know you're in here!* Izal declared, as he walked through the entrance of the cave.

*Oh, don't worry, Izal, you're going to sense me now!*

Zach's eyes flared open, ending his image of the raven walking inside the cave's entrance. With an overwhelming desire not to be found just yet, he unleashed another Blood Rush.

*There you are!* Izal called, now able to sense Zach.

"*Argh!*" Zach screamed, every muscle in his body tightening. His heart rate rose alarmingly, beating 1200 beats per minute.

*Zach! Zach, what are you doing?* Izal probed, frightened.

The young Watcher shut his eyelids, only to open them half a second later, every vein in his body bulged, as fresh blood circulated through him at an incredible rate.

"This power, it's intense!" Zach observed as he felt a whole new power surging through him.

*Zach, stop it!* Izal ordered.

"Time to see what I can do!" Zach said devilishly, turning to face Izal.

Zach started to run, faster than he had ever done, moving so fast that Izal failed to see or feel him pass.

He burst out of the cave onto the beach, and then ran up the cliff face to the level top. He could feel Izal was still inside the cave, unaware of how Zach had easily dodged him, but inside his chest, he started to feel like he was suffocating.

*What's happening?* he pondered, clutching his chest with his right hand. Never before had his heart or lungs hurt so much; pulsating so hard that it was like someone was repeatedly kicking him in the chest, knocking the wind out of him with every kick. As much as it hurt, he really needed to move. Knowing full well that in his all-powerful state, his power would easily reach Izal and give away his location.

Removing his hand from his chest, Zach began to run once more, his chosen destination none other than the Nogmal forest. His new speed did not fail him; he reached the forest in no time at all.

Zach didn't stop moving until he reached the clearing in the middle of the forest. Once there, he wasted no time in ending the Blood Rush, only to collapse onto the grass, most of his energy depleted. As he lay there gasping, he realized he had just made a mistake.

"Hello, Zach," Mako greeted him.

"Mako," Zach panted. He had been so focused on Izal and trying to evade him that he completely forgot to feel out for Mako, so he just ran directly toward him. Now he was too exhausted to evade him. For now, he would have to listen to what his former mentor had to say.

"Can you hear me?" Mako asked, concerned as he knelt down beside his former disciple.

"Yeah, I can hear you," Zach replied, getting his breathing back under control.

"You overdid it, didn't you?" Mako raised an eyebrow and locked eyes with Zach. "You used the Blood Rush." Mako stood up.

"So what?" Zach barked in reply as he stood up, just able to steady himself.

"You pushed it too far, even after I warned you about the dangers of it."

Zach's mind drifted back and he began to think about what Mako had taught him about the Blood Rush. He spoke of Watchers who had used the technique and then used it again straight away, unleashing their full potential.

Until now, everyone who had used the ability to the extent that Zach did, using it twice in a row within such a short time frame had all ended up dying, having their hearts explode. Only four previous Watchers had tried it; two had maintained it for ten minutes, whereas the other two struggled to last even one minute before succumbing to death.

It is because of the high mortality rate that Watchers in training were told by their instructors to never attempt it.

Zach was the first person to use and survive it.

"I have no idea what you're talking about," Zach lied.

"You used Blood Rush twice!" Mako exclaimed. "I told you never to do that!"

"I know," Zach smirked.

"How do you even..."

"It just came to me," Zach replied, turning away from his former master, preferring to look at the trees instead. "What do you want, Mako?" He asked bitterly.

"Judging by your tone, I take it you heard what I said last night," Mako deduced before stepping closer to Zach.

"Yes, I did, so why are you here?" Zach turned and faced his old tutor.

"Izal..."

"Told you about my power, of course he did," Zach scoffed and shrugged.

"Yes, he did, and he told me that I am wrong about you..."

"You are!" Zach snapped, his nostrils flaring and his eyes hardening. "I am a lot stronger than you think."

"Yes, I know, and Izal knows too. I was a fool to write you off so soon and Izal is right. It was I who failed you, not the other way around."

Zach said nothing.

"If you'll give me another chance, I would like to train you again."

"But maybe I don't need you anymore," Zach remarked.

Zach proceeded forward, moving away from Mako; only to then dive to the ground, roll to his right, and then side-flip off to his left. From there he leaped up onto a branch from one of the Nogmal trees and ran it along before jumping once more, this time landing one meter behind Mako.

"Maybe I'm better off training my way," Zach said.

Mako was stunned. As he turned round to face Zach, he was in awe of his new level of speed. "Whatever training you're doing..."

"It's working, I'm faster than ever." Zach boasted. "And that little display just then, I wasn't even using the Blood Rush technique." Zach flashed a maniacal smile.

"It's too much, Zach!" Mako replied.

"Too much, are you having a laugh?" Zach protested.

"However you are training, it is dangerous! It's too much too soon! You need to stop it and train with me again." Mako pleaded, his tone soft and caring.

"No thanks. If I train with you then I will never be ready for the Dark Ones, but my way, if I keep it up, then they won't be ready for me!"

"Fine, Zach, have it your way, I shall leave you to your way of training. Maybe when your common sense has returned and you've calmed down, you'll return to resume your rightful training with me. After all speed, stamina and strength are nothing without a sharp mind."

"Don't hold your breath."

"One last thing," Mako said to Zach, who had just started to walk off.

"What?" Zach asked, turning around.

"I have something for you." Mako replied with a grin, walked over to one of the trees and picked up the sword he had hidden behind it.

The sword was in its sheath; only the black handle was exposed. Embedded in the handle were a number of small rounded diamonds. The sheath was mostly black in with golden engravings on it.

Mako also picked up a loaf of bread and carried the two objects over to his former protégée.

"Firstly, I want you to have this. You must be hungry," Mako said, as he handed Zach the bread. He took it with no reluctance, his hunger way too much for him to decline the food.

"Thanks," Zach said before taking a bite of the bread.

"Good boy."

Zach looked at Mako warily.

"I also want you to have this!" Mako held out the sword for Zach to take. "You've earned it."

Forgetting about the bread, Zach reached out and took the eighty-centimeter long, single-handed arming sword. A standard military weapon of a knight and a weapon used by most Watchers.

"A sword," Zach said, as he held it up in awe. Arming swords were a favorite of his. He'd never used one, but he had marveled at Mako's collection of them for years.

Zach favored them because of how well balanced they were and the fact that they were a light, versatile weapon capable of both cut and thrust combat.

"You're giving me a sword?" Zach said as he placed his right hand on the handle and pulled it free, exposing its blade. Just like Mako's long sword, the arming sword had a black blade and it bore the Watchers mark.

"Yes I am; you've earned it. This sword marks the qualification you've earned and the completion of your exams," Mako said before taking a couple of steps back.

"And a bribe?" Zach injected suspiciously.

"A bribe it is not!" Mako snapped furiously. The elderly Watcher could not believe what Zach said. "If you truly wish to end your training with me, then fine, that's your decision..."

"Good," Zach remarked, as he slowly swung the blade, getting a feel for the sword.

"That sword is yours regardless of what you decide; I leave it in your capable hands. Just come and see me when you are ready to talk, or have made your decision, please?"

"Of course," Zach replied. Mako walked off, leaving Zach alone in the clearing.

Zach let loose a couple of practice swings before he picked the bread back up, only to suddenly sense Izal.

*Caw!*

"Great, now what?"

# CHAPTER XVI:

## *The Elohim Explanation*

*C*aw! Zach looked up in Izal's direction, unable to figure out how the bird knew where he was. *I'm already cloaking myself but Izal still knows where I am.* Then the answer came to him; it was quite obvious really. *Of course, that's it! Izal isn't sensing me here, he sensed Mako and the moment he was close enough, he was able to access Mako's mind and hear his every thought, hear his side of the conversation he had with me, hence the reason he knows I'm here.*

Zach looked down and slid the sword back in its sheath, attaching it to his belt. When he looked up, he saw Izal come into view.

"Great."

Izal soon landed on the ground in front of Zach and stared at him,

*Hello, Zach.*

*Izal.* Zach replied telepathically.

*We need to talk.*

"Later," he said out loud before turning to walk away, only to have Izal fly in front of him, blocking him.

*No, Zach, now!* Izal commanded.

"Fine," Zach sat himself down on the grassy floor in front of the bird and scowled at him. "So talk."

*You Blood Rushed.*

"So what?"

*You Blood Rushed twice.*

"Yes, I know. So does Mako. We've already had the chat about it, so no need to go over it again." Zach commented.

*You may have had a chat about it with Mako, but*

*you haven't had this chat with me.*

"Fine then," Zach scoffed.

*You have risen your entire power in less than twenty-four hours, quadrupling it in fact.*

"Yes, I have," Zach replied as he sat up. "What's wrong with that?"

*Yesterday, when I felt your true potential, it was equal to Mako's, but not now. Now I can see it has become even greater.*

"So what?" Zach questioned bluntly.

*Your sudden rise in power is down to your usage of the Blood Rush, I know it is. Somehow you have figured out how to boost your abilities at an alarming rate.*

"And?"

*How? How did you do it?*

Zach said nothing, choosing to remain silent.

*How did you raise your power so greatly?*

"A new type of training, all or nothing," Zach admitted, being half-truthful. "Besides, what has it go to do with you anyway? And why should I tell you anything? You told Mako about my power." Zach snapped, walking off.

*Mako told you that I told him?* Izal asked as he flew alongside Zach.

"Yes, he did."

*I'm sorry for betraying your confidence and trust in me by divulging your secret. I had no right.* Izal apologized.

"You're right about that!"

*But, Zach, I need to know how you improved your skills, it is important that I know.* Izal urged.

"Why?" Zach turned to look at the raven.

*Because I believe, you might be Elohim.*

"Elo what?"

*Elohim,* the bird repeated.

"And what the hell is Elohim?" Zach asked, half-interested and half-bored.

*I will tell you if you tell me exactly how you raised your power,* Izal bargained.

"Fine, you go first though." Zach pushed as he continues to walk.

*No, you first!*

"I'm improving my skills by pushing myself to my very limits and then beyond, over and over."

*By means of Blood Rush?*

"Yes."

*And that's it?*

"That's it. Simple really, now I've fulfilled my side of the deal..." Zach paused to look at the bird and smirk. "How about you start fulfilling your promise and tell me what an Elohim is."

*Not just yet. How did you do it?*

"When I was younger, Mako told me about it. He told it to me as a bedtime story and said in order to attempt it you have to have a certain level of power and be using a Blood Rush to even attempt to unlock the next level of it."

*And?* Izal probed, knowing there was more to be said.

"When I was in the cave, when you were close to finding me, I could just see it in my head, see exactly what was necessary and I went for it, I used the Blood Rush and as I used it I could feel my power inside me rising, so I let it all out," Zach confessed. "Besides, so what if the Watchers who tried it before had all died?"

*You can't use it, Zach, not like a normal Blood Rush!*

"Why not?"

*Because unlike a normal Blood Rush, the second one carries the potential of cutting your life in half, reducing the years you have to live.* Izal revealed.

"You're lying!" Zach accused.

*Am I?* The raven's green eyes gleamed.

"Yes."

*Your mind is connected to mine. Why don't you see the truth for yourself and read my thoughts.*

Looking into Izal's mind, Zach saw that there was truth in what the black bird had told him.

"Fine, I take it back. You are telling the truth." Zach said, apologizing.

*Of course I was. Now I need you to promise me something.*

"What?"

*Promise me that you will never use it again!*

At first Zach remained silent, hesitating to speak.

*Zach!*

"Fine! I promise."

*Good,* Izal replied gladly.

"So what's an Elohim?" Zach asked.

*The Elohim, which translates to mean the Shining Ones, are the true vanquishers of the Dark Ones.*

"But I thought the Children of Tormenta are the true vanquishers!" Zach said, interrupting.

*They are now, but before they came along, there were the Elohim, the Elite class of the Watchers. The best of the best, but over time they all died out.*

"Why?" Zach asked before he started walking. "Let's walk and talk."

*You walk, I'll fly,* Izal remarked before he started to flap his wings and fly overhead, circling Zach.

"So why did they all die out?" Zach rephrased his previous question.

*Old age, illness and some died in battle. They tried training others to their level, but it didn't work. Many Watchers just could not achieve their power. Time passed and the legendary Elohim became extinct.*

"That's terrible!" Zach exclaimed.

*It is a great shame, but there is an old prophecy that speaks about the return of the Shining Ones, the rise of the Elohim.*

"And you think I could be one of these Elohim?"

*It is highly possible, especially given the way you have been able to rise in power so substantially overnight,* the raven admitted.

"But I thought I was a Child of Tormenta?"

*You are. I believe you may be both.*

"Why me? Why would I be Elohim?" Zach asked, showing doubt.

*Because of what you've done, of what you can do and what you will go on to do!*

"I'm still not sure."

*Not yet, but you will be. You're a Tormenta's Child and an Elohim, one of the Shining Ones and just like the Children of Tormenta prophecy and the Elohim prophecy state, you will rise up and you will bring an end to the Shanzi,* Izal declared, armed with full faith in Zach.

"You're crazy!" Zach said disbelievingly.

*I'm anything but, and you are Elohim, Zach. That's how you know how to Blood Rush twice like that; because they did. Despite what Mako may have told you, the Elohim were the first to Blood Rush and to perform a second perfected Blood Rush that posed no damage or risk to the user,* the circling raven revealed.

"What?"

*It's true, except the Elohim didn't call it that.*

"Then what did they call it?" Zach asked.

*They called it the Grigori, or in our language, True Elohim.*

"And how do you know all of this?"

*One of these days, I will tell you, but not today.* Izal answered.

"But..."

*No.*

"Well if the Grigori is okay to use, why haven't Watchers learned how to master it? Why are they still just using the Blood Rush?"

*Only an Elohim can perform it, for it is only they who are able to perfect it. Most Watchers are unable to survive it so instead they stick with a simple Blood Rush.*

"Oh."

*Make no mistake, Zach, the Watchers are great warriors, defenders of our world, but compared to what an Elohim can do, there is no contest.*

Zach nods his understanding.

*Ah, I see you have a real sword at last; you must be eager to train with it, so I shall leave you to it. Just remember though you promised me that you wouldn't do the True Elohim, and I expect you to keep that promise.*

"You have my word," Zach replied.

*Good because I will know if you attempt it, I will sense it. See you later!* Izal flew off, above the trees and up into the sky.

Izal was right, Zach did want to practice with his sword, but not before he ate all of his bread and took a little nap.

When he woke up, he engaged in a workout that lasted until both nightfall and Shimay arrived, eager to start their next training session.

# CHAPTER XVII:

## *Shimay's New Power*

"Are you ready?" Shimay's raspy voice called out as he materialized out of thin air, appearing in front of Zach.

Unlike the night before, Shimay was wearing his hood, shielding most of his face and hiding his long, wild hair.

"I'm ready, Master," Zach replied eagerly, as he ignored the odd tingling sensation in his left arm, figuring it to be some muscle pain brought on by his workout.

"Ah, I see you have acquired a new weapon," the spirit observed, his dark eyes gazing upon the concealed weapon. His long, bony fingers bent inward as he formed a fist with his left hand.

Zach noticed the action and prepared himself for a surprise attack.

"You're not going to reply?" Shimay's chilling voice asked, making a fist with his right hand.

"Yes, I have," Zach replied, answering the spirit, moving his right foot back and taking a defensive stance.

"Good, I'm pleased you have replaced your shattered stick with the real thing." A menacing smile crossed Shimay's face. "We must find out how sharp it is, but first..." Shimay suddenly broke off.

In his moment of silence, Shimay's eyes went cold and hard, whereas Zach's mind suddenly began to tingle as a sequence of images burned its way into his thoughts. The images were all connected and bundled together and played out a scene in his head.

"Tell me, Zach..." Shimay paused, wanting to savor this moment. "Are you really ready?" Shimay asked, getting the scenario under way.

Shimay's opening comment was followed by him lashing out with his left fist, delivering a well-aimed jab to the shocked Zach, hitting him on his right cheek. The jab was then followed by a sharp right-handed uppercut before Shimay kicked Zach to the ground, only to continue his assault as he used his right leg to kick Zach's hand, reaching for his sword.

"Like I thought, you're not ready," Shimay mocked.

The scene ended with Shimay's last spoken word, leaving Zach confused over what he had just witnessed, unable to comprehend.

*What was that?* He thought to himself. *Just what did I see?*

"Tell me, Zach..." the spirit inquired, his ice-cold tone captured Zach's full attention.

*Those words, they're from those images I saw.*

"...are you really ready?" Shimay said, finishing his chilling question.

This time, he was more than ready for the phantom, so when the left fist came, Zach quickly deflected it and then chopped down on Shimay's right arm. He palm punched Shimay's right kneecap, preventing the kick that was about to come. Zach delivered a Midnight Kiss. Shimay was too surprised to even attempt to block Zach's attack, leaving him with no other option but to take the hit head on. When Zach's hands hit Shimay's torso, the spirit was blasted backward into a tree and collapsed to the ground.

When Shimay looked up, he was greeted with the sight of Zach standing over him, the sword's blade resting against the phantom's throat.

"I'd say I'm ready, yeah," Zach retorted, looking down at his fallen master.

Shimay's eyes softened and lit up with genuine pride. He smiled gladly and applauded.

"Oh bravo, well done!"

"You, you were testing me?" Zach quizzed softly.

"Of course I was, Zach; everything I do with you is a test."

"Why?" Zach asked, somewhat alarmed.

"Because if I don't, then you will never be ready for anything. Mako failed to prepare you, but I won't!" Shimay replied, knowing his words would satisfy Zach. "Now how about you lower your sword?"

"Yes, of course."

"Your speed has greatly improved since last night," Shimay noted. "You weren't even using your Blood Rush."

Zach says nothing. He knew his success was not down to his speed, but was actually due to the images he saw.

*Am I getting a new power, or is it my existing power is developing even more so?* Zach pondered, thinking if the vision he sustained was the start of a new skill, the skill of premonition.

One thing he knew for certain was that every second he spent with Shimay, his overall abilities continued to improve.

"Now, Zach, we've wasted enough time talking. We'll pick up where we left off last night. Let's find out if you can defend yourself this time around," Shimay said. "Oh, and use your sword this time. Let's see how good you are with a real blade." Shimay faded away.

Zach felt Shimay's energy appear among the trees, hiding on a branch twenty meters above him, but Shimay didn't stay still. Zach felt Shimay come hurtling at him, knocking him flat and disappearing again. There was no time to react, let alone draw his sword.

"As you have just witnessed, you are not the only one to have gotten faster," Shimay called out from his hiding spot.

"But how?" Zach gasped, as he picked himself up

and pulled his sword free.

"You."

"What?" Zach asked, twirling the sword in his hand and running over to the centre of the clearing.

"I'm faster because of you, Zach. As you improve, so do I. No matter how much stronger you get, I get stronger too and that is why I am the greatest teacher in existence!" Shimay boasted as he moved from tree to tree.

"You are a true master. Mako is nothing more than a miniscule ant that gets crushed by your mighty boots!" Zach declared.

"How very true. Now let us continue!" Shimay materialized behind Zach hoping to strike him on the back of his head. Zach easily dodged the attack.

"Very good, but do better!" Shimay commands.

Shimay chose to stay in view, remaining in the moonlit clearing and charged Zach, thrusting a palm punch of his own to the young boy's face, hitting him square on the chin before he lashed out with a left jab to Zach's stomach. And that was just the start.

Zach dodged the blows, sidestepping, ducking and kicking his attacker away. He managed to stand and pulled his sword free, parrying each blow.

"The next half hour that passed was a sparring session that saw both contenders delivering blows at increasing speeds. Just as soon as one was able to hold their own, the other had surpassed him. With each attack came escalation.

*How can this be? He must have been holding back on me!*

Zach's lack of concentration was his downfall. The spirit slammed into him at full power, causing him to drop the sword, and then threw him skyward.

Zach landed hard, the impact knocking the wind out of him. He lay there gasping for air.

"You disappoint me. I expected you to do better."

"You're just so..." Zach gasped.

"Strong, I know. I did tell you."

Zach gave in to his body's demands and lost consciousness.

"Hmm, how pitiful. No wonder Mako doubts you, you *are* weak! You're just a child, a little boy playing swordsman! Here I was believing you to be something great and yet I was so wrong. I guess Mako was right about you all along." The spirit hoped his hurtful words would seep into Zach's head and get a rise from him.

Shimay's ploy worked. Zach got up, his blue eyes hardened with rage.

"How dare you!" Zach's tone was no longer boyish, but cold, cruel and sharp, much like Shimay's. "I'll show you!" he replied as he grabbed the sword and jumped to his feet. "*Aargh!*"

Zach's scream was a scream with a purpose, a means of releasing a new wave of adrenaline as he used the Blood Rush; a Blood Rush that ended his pain and healed his wounds as a whole new energy filled him, readying him for a fight.

With his new level of power, Zach kicked the ground beneath him and thrust himself upward onto a nearby branch.

"Are you ready?" Zach asked with a new confidence, charging him with unimaginable speed. He began with kicks and jabs, and then changed over to his sword, slashing away until the phantom was forced into going invisible to avoid him.

Suddenly Shimay became visible once again. A black energy ball formed inside his right hand and he hurled it at Zach, who was just quick enough to evade it.

"Enough!" Shimay declared, taking on a solid form.

"What was that?" Zach asked, sheathing his sword.

"Just another of my many powers; but very good, Zach. I knew you could do so much better, so let us continue!" Shimay replied.

"Right!" Zach agreed, charging his master.

# CHAPTER XVIII:

## *A Rise in Power*

As the moon's rays shone upon the land, Mako was spending his time outside his home, sitting by a boulder. His legs were crossed and his hands were on his knees. He sat perfectly still, eyes closed and breathing slow, as he resided in deep meditation.

Mako felt the wind make an appearance, as a minor breeze began to blow. After a few minutes of a steady breeze, the wind intensified, wings beating through it.

"Yes, Izal?" Mako asked, unmoving.

*I'm worried,* the raven replied, landing off to Mako's right.

"About?"

*Zach.*

The Watcher opened his eyes, but instead of turning to Izal, he lifted his head up and stared at the stars dotted across the night sky. "What about him?"

*His powers are growing,* Izal answered.

"You told me that earlier," Mako replied, almost uninterested.

*Yes, but they are growing again, growing as we speak.*

"How so?" Mako turned his gaze away from the sky to Izal.

*I don't know,* Izal said. *But what I do know is that I can feel his power rising to a whole other level. I can also feel him trying to hide it, but then it spikes again.*

"He's doing the advanced Blood Rush, isn't he?" Mako asked, pacing back and forth.

*That's just it, he's not! He's only doing a normal Blood Rush, but he's improving it, pushing it to a higher level.*

"I just don't get it. Yesterday morning he was equal to my best student, but since then he has enhanced his power to become greater than the both of us. How? How did he become so much faster, stronger? And how did he learn to do the advanced Blood Rush? I can't even do it!" Mako asked, worried, firing question after question. "Just what the hell is going on round here?"

*I don't know. Maybe Zach has found a new master and has started to learn from him.*

"I beg your pardon?"

*His emotions, maybe.*

"Explain."

*Last night...*

"What about it?"

*...he heard what you thought of him. He heard your lack of faith in his skills and now he aims to prove you wrong.*

"What you're saying is that you think Zach's emotions are getting the better of him? That his hate and pride are bettering him, giving him his new-found strength and fuelling him with a new determination to become even better?" Mako asked harshly.

*Yes, I do,* Izal replied, with a small nod of the head.

"That will not do. Those two emotions can be a Watcher's enemy, if they cannot control them. Then the emotions will control the Watcher and make them careless, reckless."

*True, but then there is another reason that could explain his growth, but if this be the case, then it is not good.*

"Which is?" Mako stopped pacing and turned to face Izal. The bird's green eyes shone in the night.

*It would mean that Zach really does have another master. It would mean that there is someone else on the island and that they have found Zach and taken him on as their student, training him as they see fit.*

"And is there someone else on the island?"

*I don't believe so. At least I hope not, because if there is then I can't feel them. Besides you know as well as I do that we're not alone here.*

Mako's expression froze. "You don't think he's escaped?"

*Him? Not possible. If he has escaped then I'd feel him, unless he has found a way to hide himself from me.*

"If that is true, then we have no other choice. We will have to go inside the temple."

*Don't jump too far ahead. First we need to go to the forest, see if we can find Zach, check if he's okay.*

"And see if he is with someone." Mako added.

*That too, but then there could be another explanation for his sudden growth tonight.*

"And that is?" Mako probed.

*You gave him a sword, he could be using it and that could explain some of his newer strength.* Izal answered, offering up a possibility.

"It might explain some, but not all. Besides, do you believe that? Do you honestly believe that Zach's growth is just down to him using a sword?"

*No, I don't.*

"I thought not. We need to go to him, see the truth for ourselves. From what you've said, he could be in trouble."

*You're right.*

"We'll go now. Could you fly the both of us? Mako asked politely.

*Of course I can.* Izal said proudly.

"And you can still feel him?"

*One moment.* Izal closed his eyes and began feeling out for Zach.

"Anything?"

*Yep, got him. He's still at the clearing in the heart of*

*the Nogmal forest.*

"Then let's move out!" Mako said. The raven bowed his head and hovered above Mako.

*Hold on tight. I will be going fast.*

"Can you still feel him?" Mako asked upon landing in the forest.

*Just. He is suppressing his power, but I can just make it out.* Izal replied, following Mako. *Also, I should be the one leading, given as how I'm the one who knows where he is.*

"Just tell me which way to go," Mako said, his lips barely moving.

*Turn right and walk sixty meters.*

"One other thing," Mako whispered, ducking under a thick branch.

*What?*

"You're shielding us as well, right?"

*I am, yes, but...*

"But what?"

*With Zach's skills developing the way they are, it is highly possible that his abilities have grown to the point where he can feel us regardless.*

"Is that possible?"

*Yes.*

"Then let us hope that it has not come to that," Mako whispered.

*Maybe I should project our own energy to be back up at the house, so if he does sense us, he'll feel us there instead.*

"You can do that?" Mako was unaware that Izal could do such a trick.

*Yes.*

"What about Zach, can he project his energy?" Mako asked, thinking that if Zach could do the same, then he could be projecting his life-force at this very minute.

*No,* Izal replied, projecting their presence elsewhere.

"No?" Mako repeated. "No because he can't do it? Or no because..."

*No, because I never tried to teach it to him.*

"Why not?"

*So he could never use it against me.*

Mako nodded, understanding.

*Up ahead,* Izal announced, spotting Zach in the centre of the open area amongst the trees, swinging his sword from side to side.

Mako followed Izal's gaze and looked into the clearing where Zach was bathed in the glow of moonlight. He appeared to be alone.

"Can you see anyone with him?" Mako whispered.

*No, I can't,* Izal replied, keeping his sights fixed on Zach.

Zach thrust out with his blade and swung upward.

"Can you feel anyone?"

*No, nothing! There is nothing else here.*

"Are you sure?"

*Positive.*

Both man and raven turned their attention back to Zach, who continued to perfect his sword skills.

"We're going to the temple," Mako whispered. "Something just doesn't feel right. We need to go check things out."

*As you wish,* Izal agreed, and then lightly joked. *Do you remember where the entrance is? And how to get to it?*

"Of course I do."

*And judging by the fact that you said "we're," I take it you would like me to come with as opposed to staying here to keep an eye on Zach?*

Mako pondered the question. "Hmm? I'll need you to come with me, besides Zach can look after himself." Without another word, both man and bird left the forest.

# CHAPTER XIX:

## *Shimay's Story*

Using his own powers, Zach was able to see through Izal's projection trick and felt both Mako's and Izal's presence. Zach felt his former mentors making their way to the forest, as he was training with Shimay; he issued a warning to the spirit that they would have company.

Shimay quickly made his escape and left his student on his own.

He decided to keep practicing for another five minutes after he felt his old masters left, just in case they decided to sneak back. When they didn't, he put his sword away and strolled over to a Nogmal tree. This tree was much wider than those nearby and much darker in color.

Zach smiled and rapped his knuckles on the tree, knocking four times.

"It's safe to come out!" Zach called out, taking two steps back.

Suddenly the tree began to move, shuddering and swaying, shrinking down to a mere human form.

"That really is an amazing trick. Any chance you can teach me how to do that?" Zach asked in awe as the tree turned into the Spirit of Iris.

"Sadly I cannot, not while you are still breathing." Shimay replied in his cold voice. "I cannot teach the tricks of the dead to those still living."

"I understand," Zach replied glumly.

"Now let us get on with your training. Sunrise will soon be upon us."

"But..." Zach protested.

"But what?" Shimay's eyes hardened.

"You said you were murdered and that you used to

be the Guardian of Iris."

"Yes, and?"

"I want to know the story, the full story."

Shimay clicked his tongue and smiled. "I am sorely tempted to decline your request; however I am willing to tell you my tale provided you accept my deal."

"What sort of deal?" Zach asked, uneasiness setting in.

"I will do you a favor by telling you my story and in return you will owe me a favor and when I make my request, you are obliged to say yes." Shimay's eyes narrowed as he stared at Zach, his gaze hard and cold. "So tell me, do you want to make a deal? Do you still want to hear my story?"

"I do," Zach answered calmly, not even taking a second to think about the potential danger Shimay's favor could entail.

"And you accept the deal?"

"I do."

"Good, but first you must prove yourself. Prove yourself worthy to even listen to my tale."

"What must I do?"

"Your speed continues to improve, but I want to see just how fast you have become. If you can catch me, then I will tell you my story, but if you can't, then I won't."

"Catch you, that's it?" Zach was a little unsure. The challenge seemed easy enough.

"That's it," Shimay replied casually.

"It's that..." Zach stopped in mid-speech due to him losing sight of Shimay, who had just used his speed to escape. "...simple," he said, finishing his sentence glumly. "Of course not. *Aargh!*" he roared, unleashing yet another Blood Rush.

Zach knew full well that his best chance of catching the ghost was in his enhanced state, and took off after the spirit.

The game of cat and mouse went all over the island, starting in the forest only to move up to the Watcher's Summit, and then back down to the western side of the island. Zach chased Shimay around the vegetable plots where Mako grew fresh food, and followed him through the rocky valley, past small ruins, only to have Shimay lead him away, down to the beach.

With the ability of flight, Shimay was able to hold Zach off and narrowly dodge him, but the longer the chase went on, the faster Zach became and as his speed went up, so did his sensory abilities, which enabled him to receive another vision showing Shimay's next few moves, giving Zach the ultimate advantage.

Returning to the clearing, Zach captured Shimay, leaping straight at the solid spirit, knocking him to the dirt.

"Got you!" Zach rasped between heavy breaths, sitting on Shimay's chest.

"So you have," Shimay smiled. "So how about you let me up and we'll begin my story."

"Yes, sir." Zach beamed as he helped Shimay to his feet, then sat down in the dirt, eager to hear.

"My story dates back over three hundred years, back to a time when my name was Iris. I was named before this island, which was actually renamed in my honor," Shimay revealed.

"What was it called before?" Zach asked.

"Isla de Shanzi."

"Shanzi, as in..."

"The Dark Ones, yes. You see, before the Watchers had come along and claimed this island, the Shanzi had it first. The Shanzi Temple, the home of the Shanzi King, was in the centre of the volcano."

"The Shanzi King?" Zach asked.

"Yes, the Shanzi King, Lord Darkari, ruler of the Mares Realm. Now, as a young newly graduated Watcher and a Child of Tormenta, it was my duty to free Mares and the other Realms, so I came to this Realm and freed every island from Darkari's control."

"Every island?"

"Every island, including this one, which I saved last. It was quite the challenge, but I saved it nonetheless and defeated most of the Shanzi that occupied this land."

"Most?"

"Yes, most. You see, sadly I was not able to destroy all of the Shanzi. A few of them were too strong to be destroyed, including Lord Darkari," the phantom admitted bitterly.

"Then if they didn't get destroyed, what did you do to them?"

"I used a technique that I learned during my travels and used it to open up a portal to another world, a world unlike this one, and banished them into it. I forced them into the portal and sealed them inside, ridding this world of them forever. The Mares Realm was now free from evil, as were the rest of the Realms in all of Oceania and so because of my valiant efforts, the Isle of Iris came to be and I choose to make it my home, the home of the new Mares Guardian," Shimay said proudly.

"Then what happened?"

"I lived out my days on the island as a teacher, educating future Watchers, but then *he* came along."

"The student who killed you?" Zach guessed.

"Yes, the student who killed me. He had come to the island in the same way that you had done, as a baby in a basket, and like you, he was a Child of Tormenta. For over twenty years he was a dedicated student, the best I ever taught, and on the day of his twenty-first birthday, it was time for him to begin his journey out into the world."

"Then what happened?"

"I continued my role as a mentor, teaching all those who would wash up on this island, but none of the students were like him, as hard as I taught them. They never got anywhere near his level." Shimay looked down to the ground, halting his tale, his eyes misting over as he envisioned his past before resuming.

"Twenty-seven years passed, with him off having adventures, battling monsters, taking on many evils. Then came the day his adventures ended, and he returned to the Isle of Iris, desiring to bring about my demise!"

"How did it happen? How did he kill you?" Zach asked.

"A sword fight. We battled and he lost. I disarmed him and showed him mercy. He got the upper hand and stabbed me in the back as I tried to walk away, but stabbing me wasn't enough for him."

"What happened next? What did he do?"

"He grabbed me by my legs and began dragging my body..."

"That's terrible!" Zach gasped.

"Yes, it was," Shimay replied. "He dragged my body across the island and over to the tunnel that goes deep inside the heart of the volcano, he dragged me through the tunnel and opened up the Shanzi Temple, where he then dumped me inside, locking me up as I lived out my last few moments. Ever since then my spirit has haunted the temple as I was unable to escape it until..."

"Until what?"

"Until I grew strong enough to escape and began my life on this island. I have tried to leave but sadly, I cannot."

"Why not?"

"The manner in which I died."

"Your murder?" Zach injects.

"Yes, my murder," Shimay answered bitterly. "Because of the way I was betrayed by my best student, I am forced to remain trapped here, imprisoned until my story was told and I become strong enough to lift the barrier keeping me here."

"So now you should be able to move on?" Zach probed, jumping to his feet. "You've told me your story and surely you're more than powerful enough now, enough to break the barrier."

"Not quite," Shimay replied. "I still have some way to go yet."

"Is there anything I can do?"

"Maybe you can," the spirit answered.

"What?"

"You can lend me your powers, your strength."

"Pardon?"

"You could lend me your powers, Zach." The phantom said, looking at the boy with a hopeful smile.

"What would that do?" Zack questioned, starting to feel nervous for some reason unknown to him.

"It would give me the power I would need to lift the barrier.

"Would it?"

"Yes, it would."

"How do you know?"

"Because you are all powerful and only your power can set me free."

"Then I'll help you, anyway I can, and we can lift it together," Zach replied with a grin.

"I'm afraid that will not work. The task is mine alone, but I cannot do it if I don't have your powers," Shimay said.

"I'm not sure," Zach said, fearing the danger it could put him in.

"But you owe me, Zach. We made a deal."

"I'll do anything, *anything* but this," Zach replied.

"But this is all I require; I need and desire nothing else. Please help me, Zach!" Shimay pleaded.

"I'm… I'm not sure."

"It's just a loan. As soon as I am done with your power, I swear I will return it to you." Shimay promised, hoping to reassure Zach and get him on his side.

"Okay, I'll do it," Zach said. "Tell me what you need me to do."

"I need you to activate your Blood Rush," Shimay instructed.

"I'm doing it right now. From the moment I activated it to catch you, I haven't stopped using it." Zach disclosed happily.

"Okay, good. I'll need you to charge it up though, push it as far as you can. Can you do that for me?"

"Certainly."

"Good. While you're doing that, I'll be absorbing your power and I'll need you to give me everything. This won't work otherwise," Shimay said.

"As you wish."

"Very well then, we shall begin. Come to me." the spirit commanded.

Zach did, getting down on his knees. Shimay placed his right hand on Zach's scruffy hair.

"Good, now focus your power!" Shimay ordered.

Zach roared as he allowed his powers to spike, letting his energy flow.

Shimay's hand began to glow a bright purple as the energy flowed from Zach and surged into him.

"Good, good! Keep it coming!"

"*Aargh!*" Zach screamed, as more of his power was passed over.

"My, oh my, this power is exceptional. Don't stop!" Shimay cried out loud. He could feel his own powers growing as they mixed perfectly with Zach's.

The purple glow coming from Shimay's hand grew in size. In mere seconds, the purple energy covered them both.

"Oh, oh yes!" the phantom exclaimed. "Oh yes, Zach, keep it coming, do not stop!" Shimay commanded.

"I won't!" Zach whispered, feeling incredibly

drained, already having passed over three quarters of his power.

"Just a little more!" Shimay ordered.

"I'm trying!" Zach cried.

Suddenly the purple energy that enveloped both Zach and Shimay disappeared completely. Zach collapsed to the ground, barely breathing.

"Out already? That is a shame, I'd have preferred it to last a little longer, but I have more than enough power now and that is all thanks to you, Zach." Shimay said, feeling his new powers coursing through him, feeling as if he had the strength of gods.

"You're free now, right? Free to destroy the barrier?" Zach asked, still lying spent on the ground.

"There is no barrier, Zach. I lied!"

"What?" Zach whispered, horrified.

"Thanks to you, I now have all power I need."

"And what are you going to do with it?" Zach asked.

"I'm going to get my long awaited revenge and kill the man who killed me." Shimay's black eyes took on a soulless appearance.

"What?" Zach asked. "Who?"

"Your precious Master Mako, of course."

"What?" Zach was completely stunned.

"It was he who killed me, but after two centuries of waiting, I can now bring about his demise."

"You're crazy! Mako can't have killed you, he's far too young!"

"Actually, it might surprise you to know this, but Mako is two hundred and fifty-three years old, but with this new power of mine, he will not live to see another day."

"You...you deceived me, used me!" Zach groaned as he lay useless on the ground, exhausted, powerless to do anything.

"Yes, I did and I enjoyed it and now is the time that

I kill both Mako and Izal. Who knows, maybe after I've done that, I'll reopen the Shanzi Temple and let out the imprisoned."

"What? No! Why would you do that? Why release the Shanzi?"

"Why not, Zach? Your kind have had this world long enough; maybe it's time that the Shanzi get their turn with it. Evil will walk free, but to prevent you from ruining my plans, it's time you died. Goodbye, young Watcher." Shimay raised his hand and fired a ball of energy at Zach. Unable to counter the blow, his heart stopped upon impact.

Shimay went off in search of Mako.

# CHAPTER XX:

## *The Morning Star*

Just a few minutes before sunrise, before Shimay had drained Zach, Mako and Izal were walking inside a tunnel, which traveled deep inside the volcano to the temple. Having checked it, they were now walking toward daylight.

*Well, it's not been opened,* Izal said, breaking the silence.

"Not since I opened it to leave Iris to die in there," Mako replied.

*And without the key, there is no way in,* Izal remarked, spotting the end of the tunnel up ahead. In less than five minutes they would be outside once again.

"I just hope the key is safe," Mako said.

*Wait!* Izal shouted stopping in his tracks as Mako strolled past him.

Mako turned to look at his companion. "What is it?"

*I can feel something,* Izal answered.

The raven felt a huge source of power emitting from the forest.

At first, he felt just the one presence, but as he focused on it, he realized that there were actually two. Two life forces that are equal in power, but suddenly one of the life forces began to weaken, a life force Izal knew all too well. Zach was diminishing, and quickly.

"Izal, what is it?" Mako questioned.

*It's Zach, he's in the forest, but he's not alone!*

"What do you mean, he's not alone?" Mako asked, alarmed.

*I mean someone is with him and whoever it is, they are powerful, very powerful. And they're stealing from him.*

"Stealing what?"

Izal felt the aura of Zach's companion and what he could read was pure evil, an evil that blasted Zach, causing his life force to vanish altogether.

"Stealing what?" Mako repeated.

*I can't feel him. He's gone!*

"You mean he's hiding his power again?" Mako probes, hoping that Izal's answer would be yes.

*No, Mako, he's dead! His life force was stolen!* Izal cried in anguish.

"What do you mean dead?" Mako exclaimed.

*I mean he's dead! Whomever he was with, they have just killed him.*

"Then we shall avenge him!" Mako replied with murder in mind, pulling his sword out, torn between grief and rage.

*No, Mako! Wait!* Izal shouted. He could feel the mysterious force responsible for Zach's death coming to them.

"Why?" Mako shouted.

*Zach's killer, he's...* Izal started to warn, just as Shimay came into view at the entrance of the tunnel.

"Right in front of you!" Shimay said coldly.

"Iris," Mako scowled, recognizing the spirit.

"Actually, it's Shimay now," the Spirit of Iris remarked with a cruel grin and stepped into the tunnel, closing the gap between him and Mako.

"Of course it is," Mako replied calmly. *Stay behind me, Izal.* Mako conversed in thought.

"You don't look so happy to see me, Mako!" Shimay taunted.

*Mako, be careful.*

*I will.*

"I don't recall you being this quiet when you were younger," the spirit observed, noticing Mako's continued silence. "You must be talking to your bird."

"What are you doing here Shimay? I thought I…"

"Killed me? Oh you did, but you see, my desire for revenge is far too great for me to just leave this island, therefore anchoring me to this world, this island and to you!"

"And how did you escape the temple? I buried your body in there so you could rot with all your Shanzi friends."

"That's easy, really. You may have locked me in, but the seal placed on the temple was created to prevent Shanzi from escaping. It wasn't designed to stop Watchers or ghosts from escaping, and being both, I was able to walk straight through it with no problem at all."

"Tell me, Shimay, before you realized that the seal wouldn't prevent you from escaping, how long did it take you to figure it out?" Mako probed, smiling dangerously at him.

"I'll admit it took me some time."

"How much time?"

"Let's just say that I've only been on this side of the seal for the last fifty-three years," the phantom replied.

Mako started to laugh.

*No, Mako! Don't!* Izal warned, knowing full well that Mako's laughter was only fuelling Shimay's hatred of him.

"Hmm, your mocking of me simply will not do, so I'm going to kill you now. And don't fret, Izal, you will be next!" Shimay cried evilly just before he charged at Mako, who was quick to lash out.

His move was a wasted effort for Shimay. He grabbed the sword from Mako's hands, tossing it outside the tunnel.

*Run, Mako!* Izal pleaded, knowing Shimay was far superior. In a bid to save Mako, he flew at the spirit, jabbing at him, giving the Watcher a chance to escape. But Mako didn't leave.

Shimay grabbed Izal by the throat and knocked him out, tossing his body aside.

"Stupid bird!" Shimay growled.

"That bird is my friend..." Mako paused, grabbing Shimay and driving him rapidly outside, up out of the tunnel. "For Izal and Zach!"

On the western side of the island, the sky lit up, bright oranges, yellows and reds merging with the blue sky, as the sun began its rise.

Shimay landed on a rock pillar.

Izal had recovered and flew over to Mako's sword.

"You'll pay for that, Mako," Shimay threatened. "You may have some fight in you, but thanks to your student, I have more than enough power to destroy the both of you," Shimay boasted, preparing to make another dark energy ball.

"You're right, but you forget one thing," Mako remarked.

"And what's that?"

*Sword,* Mako ordered. Izal swooped in with the blade in his beak, with the hilt pointed toward Mako's hand.

Mako held the weapon above his head, letting the rising sun shine its rays down onto the blade.

*Do it!* Izal urged.

"And what's that?" Shimay repeated, as his energy ball grew in size.

"I'm the Guardian of Iris and with the help of Lucifer, the Morning Star, I banish you to the prison you came from!"

Upon saying the words "Morning Star," Mako's sword lit up, bathed in a golden glow brought on by the sun. All Shimay could do was look on in horror.

"This will not kill you, but it will contain you long enough for me to discover a means of destroying you once and for all."

Mako swung his weapon, letting the golden vertical beam shoot straight into Shimay and blast him down the tunnel, through the seal, and into the Shanzi Temple, locking him away.

Both Izal and Mako stood looking at the temple. Mako kept a firm grip on the sword just in case.

*He's gone, sealed inside the temple,* Izal said.

"You sure?" Mako questioned.

*Positive.* Izal answered, able to feel Shimay safely contained.

Deeply saddened, Mako said, "We'd best go find Zach. The least we can do is give him a decent burial."

*You're right. I'll fly us, it's quicker.*

Upon landing in the open area, Mako immediately spotted Zach.

"You're positive he's dead?" he asked, kneeling down beside Zach and placing his hand on the boy's chest.

*Yes.* Izal answered.

"His heart!" Mako exclaimed, turning to look at Izal.

*What about it?* Izal quizzes.

"It's beating!" Mako said. He leaned his ear against the boy's chest, listening intently.

*No, he can't be alive, I'd feel it.* Izal replied with conviction.

"He is alive. Not only is his heart beating, but he is using the Blood Rush."

*Mako, get back!* Izal warned. *I can feel him, he's energy is back. You're right, he is alive!*

Mako looked to Izal and then back to Zach. His heartbeat had returned to normal. He opened his eyes and looked dazedly around him. "Where am I?" he whispered, and collapsed again.

"Let's get him back to the house, get him in his bed," Mako said.

*Good idea.*

Mako scooped Zach up in his arms.
*He'll be okay, right?* Izal asked.
"I honestly don't know," Mako answered.

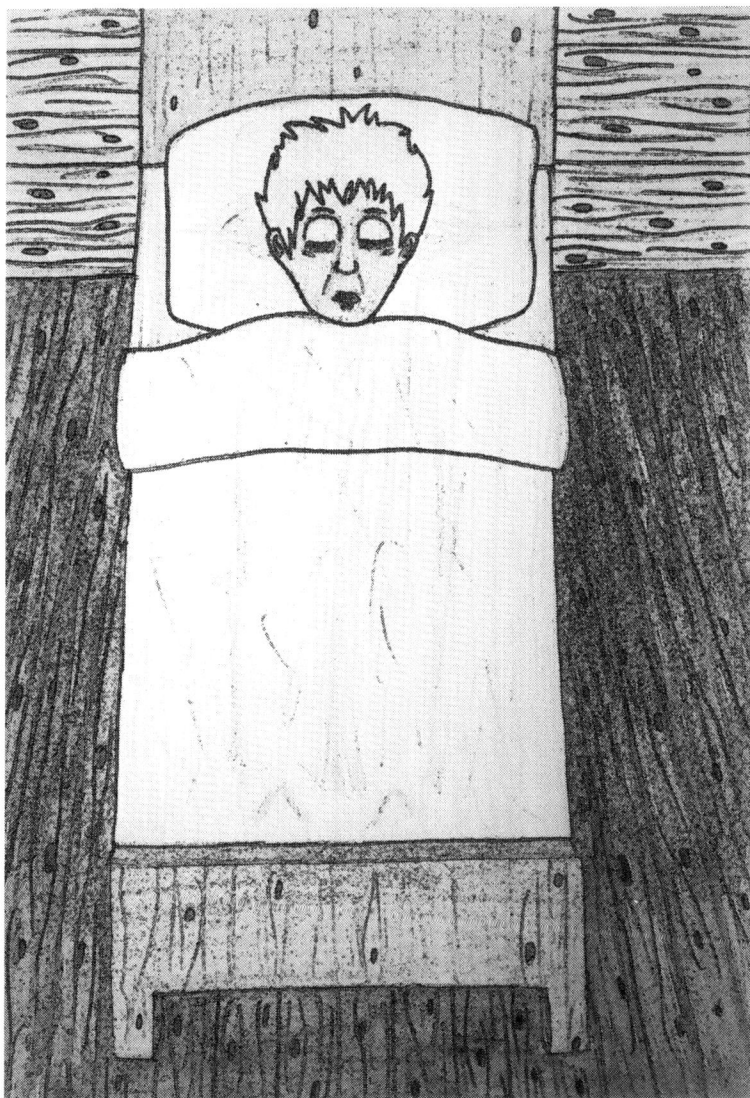

# CHAPTER XXI:

## *Forgotten Memories*

Two days passed and Mako and Izal were still waiting for Zach to regain consciousness.

*Still nothing,* Izal said. Ever since Zach's energy returned, it remained at the same level as when they revived him. It was Mako's belief that Zach's power would increase prior to awaking.

"And what about Iris?" Mako questioned.

*You mean Shimay?*

"Yeah, Shimay. Any change there?"

*He's still in the temple. The series of seals you put in place are holding, for now, but they will not remain for long. He will return and when we does, we need to be ready. Have you discovered a means of defeating him yet?*

"Sadly, I have not," Mako replied, looking down at the big book on his lap.

The leather-bound book, penned all in the Wikita language, the main language of the Indiania realm, was opened to a page containing writings about spirits and ghosts. Mako hoped to find something, but after failing to do so, he slammed the book shut.

*So, no spells or enchantments we can use then?* The raven asked, casting his mind backward and thinking about the people of Indiania. A race of various beings all gifted with magic, be they magicians, witches, wizards, warlocks, sorcerers, sorceresses and even elves. Being as gifted as they were, many an Indianian took to penning various spell books.

Despite being a swordsman and being born magically un-equipped, like most Oceanians, Mako had a deep interest in all things magical and possessed quite an impressive magical library.

"Not in any of the books I have in my collection. We might have to do this the old way."

*By old way, you mean a Power Play?* Izal asked.

"Yes," Mako answered.

*You do realise of course that for a Power Play to work, you have to be as strong as, or close enough to, the one you are challenging. I hate to say it, Mako, but you are nowhere near close enough.*

"I am well aware, yes." Mako answered.

*Then what good is a Power Play? You are at your capacity; there is no going beyond that.*

"Not if I can do an advanced Blood Rush."

*Only then could you possibly be strong enough to at least chance it. Besides it's pointless covering all this, especially since you can't.*

"Then I'll learn," Mako snapped.

*Then you will fail.*

"Then at least I tried to do something. What would you have me do?"

*You? Nothing. But Zach, he can beat Shimay,* Izal answered, having every faith in the boy.

"Zach? Zach, who is unconscious and powerless?"

*All of that is true and yes, as it stands he has no real power, and still in a coma, but as you have learned, Zach is more than capable of raising his power in almost no time at all. I know he can do it again. I know he can destroy Shimay.*

"Oh you *know* it, do you?" Mako questioned harshly, scanning the pages again.

*Yes, I do!*

"What about waking him up? Do you know how to do that too?"

*Actually, I think I do, but first maybe you should check your books for any spell or enchantment we can use to wake him.*

"I have, many times!" Mako snapped. "And unless we have the aid of an Indiania priestess to cast the spell, there is nothing we can possibly do besides wait it out. I can't see a priestess in here, can you?"

*Fine then, I guess you leave me no choice. I do have one idea that might work.*

"And what's that?" Mako asked, setting the book aside.

*You are going to Blood Rush and attempt to kill Zach.*

"What do you mean, attempt to kill him?"

*Well, if I'm wrong, you will kill Zach, but if I am right, and I believe I am, your blade won't even touch him.*

"What do you mean?"

*I'm not divulging anything else; you either do it or you don't!*

"And if I do, what's the success rate for your idea?"

*One percent.*

"One percent? Just a measly one percent?" Mako asked, arching a lone eyebrow.

*Yes.*

"That's good enough for me," said Mako. He took his sword in hand and readied himself to strike.

*Don't forget the Blood Rush,* Izal said, getting out of the way.

"I won't."

Mako closed his eyes and exhaled slowly. Then he allowed his heart rate to accelerate, succumbing to a Blood Rush.

*Do it! Do it now!*

"Zach, please know that if this doesn't work, then I am deeply sorry."

His swing was powerful and his aim true. Zach vanished under the blow, the sword slicing through his bed.

"Is this some kind of training exercise that I don't know about?" Zach asked from the floor, his own heart going at six hundred beats per minute.

Even unconscious, Zach's senses had been aware of the impending danger and his body reacted instinctively by going into a Blood Rush.

"No Zach, it's not, it's..." Mako attempted to come up with a reasonable and believable answer.

*It's, it's er...* Izal also attempted to answer Zach's question but he too was unable to do so.

"It's what?" Zach inquired, his eyes drifting back and forth between his two tutors.

"You've been in a coma for the last couple of days," Mako said, sheathing his sword.

"So you thought you would kill me?" Zach cried.

*Not kill you, but attempt to do so as a means to wake you up.*

"Attempt? You mean you weren't even sure if it would work?"

*We were desperate; we still are!*

"Why are you desperate?" Zach scratched his head.

"Because there is a vengeful spirit on the island who tried to kill all of us, and thanks to you, who aided him by giving him your powers, he is more powerful than ever and if Izal's beliefs are true, only you can kill him."

"What? Who?"

"Your friend Shimay! Your new mentor, who you spent the last two nights training with before you then transferred all your newfound powers over to, just before he killed you. Well, tried to."

Zach looked at Mako like he'd lost his mind. "What are you talking about?"

"Stop playing games!" Mako barked scornfully.

"*I'm not!*" Zach cried, throwing his arms up in frustration.

With growing curiosity, Izal decided to look inside Zach's mind.

"You are!"

*No, he's not!* Izal confirmed. *You poor boy. You poor, poor boy.*

"Izal, what are you on about?" Zach asked.

Izal looked to Mako. *His memory has been wiped.*

"What do you mean, wiped?" Mako asked.

Izal had already turned back to Zach. *What is the last thing you remember?*

"Shooting arrows in the forest just after I passed my examination," Zach replied.

"You don't remember anything else?" Mako asked.

"No, nothing," Zach replied, trying to remember more, but unable to.

*I'm curious. If you can't remember anything after your little bow and arrow session, how do you think you got back here?*

"I must have gotten tired and passed out and then you or Mako must have come looking for me since I didn't come back here on my own. However that obviously isn't the case because according to the two of you, I've been in a coma."

"I don't understand it. How can your memories be gone? Do you have any ideas?" Mako directed his question to the black bird.

*I may have an idea. On the night Shimay took your powers, or you transferred them over to him, he tried to kill you and although I did feel you die, when we found you, your heart was beating and your life force had returned.*

"So?" Zach interjected.

*When we found you, and you had made your return to the land of the living, you were using the advanced Blood Rush technique.*

"What? I can't…"

*Actually you can. During your training with Shimay, you learned how to master it.*

Mako turned to face his student, who, thanks to the memory loss, no longer remembered overhearing Mako's doubt in him.

"I can actually do it?" Zach asked in amazement.

"Yes, you can," remarked Mako. "Now let Izal continue with his thoughts as to how you are still alive and how you lost your memory."

"Of course," Zach nodded.

*I think Zach must have used the advanced Blood Rush technique just as Shimay tried to kill him. It is my theory that after transferring your powers that you were on the verge of passing out, but as Shimay's attack was about to claim your life, your heart rate climbed to 1200 beats per minute as a new wave of energy was released and the killer blow dealt. Now given as how the technique was used at such a life and death moment, the energy released was so great that Shimay's attack wasn't strong enough to kill him, but more than strong enough to erase Zach's memory and shield his life force for a short period of time.*

"Plausible, I guess," Mako said, "but I'm not quite convinced. You have more knowledge in this area then I do. Have you ever heard of things like this before?"

*There have been some stories that I've read; stories about Elohim, who did cheat death by going Grigori.*

"Yes, but like you said, they're stories and Zach is not Elohim. He can't be; the Shining Ones are no more."

"What's Elohim?" Zach asked.

*Maybe he's not, maybe he is.*

"Forget about how he lost his memory; let's discuss getting it back. Can his memory return? Is there something we can do to bring back what is gone?"

*There is a block, a dark cloud in his head burying his memories. Sadly, I don't have the ability or the know-how to free his thoughts but I do know someone who might be able to help.*

"What are Elohim?" Zach asked again.

"Will it work?" Mako asked.

*It is worth a try.*

"Then go, go see whoever it is you know and do not come back until you have a solution for us."

*And what are you going to do?*

"I'm going to train Zach, get him ready for his battle with Shimay."

"What are Elohim?" Zach asked again. This time, they gave him their attention.

"Elohim are an old race of warriors who died out a long time ago," Mako answered. "Now forget about the Elohim, Zach. We have more important matters to deal with, like getting your memory back and the fact that there is a spirit on this island that wants the three of us dead and you are our only hope of stopping him."

"Yes, Master," Zach replied.

"We shall commence your training in one hour, but first Izal and I need to discuss his journey. Get cleaned up and get something to eat."

Without another word, Mako and Izal left the room, leaving Zach to his tasks.

# CHAPTER XXII:

## *Bidding Farewell*

One hour passed and Zach was outside, standing face on with one of Mako's training posts, striking it with one of the old wooden swords that he had taken from his bedroom. Due to the memory loss, he had forgotten that Mako upgraded him to metal.

Despite the sun being in his eyes, Zach struck hard and true at the post, giving the exercise his full concentration.

"Zach! Have you got a minute?" Mako called from the doorway. Coming outside with Izal, he concealed the arming sword behind his back.

"Coming!" Zach struck one last blow and ran to him.

"Where's your sword?" Mako probed, looking down at the wooden one held tightly in Zach's hand.

"Right here," the boy exclaimed, waving it.

"That's not your sword," Mako stated. Izal started looking at Zach in a strange way.

"What do you mean it's not my sword?"

"No, *this* is your sword," Mako said, bringing the weapon out from behind his back and extending it to Zach. "I bestow upon you this sword to commemorate your promotion to Watcher's apprentice."

"It's mine?" Zach asked excitedly, placing the wooden sword on the ground and reaching out for the object in Mako's hands.

"It's yours," Mako answered with a happy grin.

As Zach took it in his own hands, he pulled the weapon free of its sheath, exposing the blade, and was instantly in awe.

"It's beautiful," he said, proceeding to gaze admiringly at it.

"Yes it is, but it is very important that you use it as much as you can. Practice with it because, as you know, practice makes perfect." Mako said.

"I will," vowed Zach, putting the blade away and tying the sheath to his belt.

"Now, Izal will soon be leaving us, in the hopes he can find a means to unlock your memories, but he has told me that even though you are much stronger than you realize. You are still capable of raising your power at an exceptional rate, so when we start training, it will be the most intense thing you have ever done. Do you understand?"

"Yes sir," Zach answered, turning to Izal.

*Impressive,* the raven commented.

"What's impressive?" Mako asked.

*Zach's body, even though his mind has forgotten, his body hasn't.*

"What do you mean?"

*His body remembers all the training he did.*

"How?" Zach asked.

*You're using a Blood Rush,* Izal said.

"And?" Mako asked.

*When we attempted to behead him, Zach had used the Blood Rush technique to escape your blade and he hasn't stopped. He's kept it going this entire time.*

"Really?" Zach asked, unaware of the fact that he was still using the technique.

Mako asked, "Are you sure?"

*Positive. Not only can I sense it, I can actually hear his heart beating the six hundred beats per minute.*

"Cool," Zach remarked. He couldn't help but grin and nod his head in satisfaction. "Do you want me to stop it?" he asked, directing his question toward Mako.

"Do you need to?" his master enquired in return.

"No," Zach answered bluntly.

"Then keep it going," Mako replied curiously, not even bothering to take a second to think whether Zach should or shouldn't. "Let's see just how long you can maintain it for."

"Okay," Zach grinned.

"Now, Zach, Izal is going to leave us for a while on some business. For how long I do not know. So it is just going to be us for a while." Mako stroked Izal's head affectionately. So say your goodbye and we can commence your training."

"Take care, Izal," Zach said, bidding farewell and wrapping his arms around the raven, giving him a hug.

*You too, Zach,* replied Izal. *Just remember that whatever Mako throws at you, you can take it and dish it back twofold. Do not hold back; it's all or nothing, understand?*

"Yes," Zach replied, going back to the practice post.

Left with Izal, Mako said his own farewell.

"Izal..."

*Mako.*

"Fly safe and I wish you success in your efforts."

*I shall do my best, but please be careful. Shimay could escape from the temple any second now.*

"I am aware of that," Mako affirmed.

*I mean it; be prepared. He will return and when he does, you need to be ready.*

"I know." Mako replied, watching Zach slashing at the target with his sword.

*I mean it, you and Zach need to be ready!*

"And we will be."

*Good.* Izal looked skyward and saw dark clouds forming. *I'd best be off before the rain comes.*

"Of course. Goodbye, Izal."

*Goodbye.*

Without another word or thought exchanged, Izal

beat his wings and took off, gaining height as he headed south. Zach stopped slashing the target and ran to the edge of the volcano, where he watching the raven depart.

"'Bye, Izal!'"

*Caw!*

*Goodbye, Zach!*

"Are you ready, Zach?" Mako asked, unsheathing his sword.

"Ready for what?" Zach questioned, keeping his eyes to the sky.

Mako charged him from behind and was just about to swing his sword only to see Zach suddenly vibrate on the spot before disappearing altogether. With his student gone, Mako lowered his blade and looked all around him.

"Zach?" he called out. He was answered by the touch of Zach's sword at his throat.

"Right here!" Zach said, holding the blade steady.

"Very good, Zach," Mako comments. "Especially since your powers are actually weaker than the last time we drew swords."

"It's like Izal said, my mind may not be able to remember the power I had aspired to, but my body sure does and so when I act upon instinct, my body allows me to move at my true speed."

"That's perfectly understandable, Zach, but you forgot something," Mako remarked, as he readied himself for his next move.

"And what's that?" Mako disappeared and then reappeared behind Zach with his sword against his student's throat.

"Instincts alone are not enough." Mako retorted.

Zach lashed out with a quick backward kick with his left leg, hitting Mako in his left knee, ducking under his master's sword and taking two steps back.

"Hmm, I'm glad to see you still maintain your cunning. You're going to need it," the older Watcher commented before he lunged at Zach, who sidestepped the move and swung his own weapon high in an attempt to get behind Mako, only to have the seasoned swordsman easily dodge the blow.

Annoyed that he missed his master, he lashed out again, swinging at all angles, but even then his six swings did no good as Mako deflected them all.

"Not bad, but do better!" Mako commanded.

"Fine, I will!" Zach remarked as he ducked under a swing delivered by his tutor, only to then put his weapon away.

"You will want that," Mako commented.

"Maybe, maybe not."

Zach charged at Mako only to fade away and blur into view as he moved round, only stopping when presented with an opportunity to strike. He lashed out with a right-handed palm punch to Mako's spine, followed by a quick kick to the back of his master's legs, forcing him to face plant on the ground.

Mako quickly rolled onto his back, only to have Zach stomp on his right wrist, his sword hand. Mako let go of his sword, Zach snatched it up and held it with both hands.

Suddenly disinterested in the practice session, Zach moved away from Mako, who got to his feet as Zach engaged in a couple of swings before he drew his own sword and compared the difference in weight and balance.

"Not bad," Mako commented. "In fact I'm quite impressed, but I doubt you'll be able to do that again."

"You sure about that?" Zach quizzed.

"I guess we'll find out."

"Here's your sword back," Zach said, tossing Mako's sword back to him.

Mako caught it, and also got caught by Zach charging him, knocking him to the ground once again.

"This training doesn't seem too hard to me," Zach

remarked as he stood back up.

Mako also rose and looked straight at his student. "Zach, we're just getting started."

# CHAPTER XXIII:

## *Izal's Return*

A fortnight passed; two full weeks of intensive training and Izal had yet to return. For Zach, the majority of the last fourteen days was spent engaging in sword fight after sword fight, some lasting up to four hours and some only three seconds as Mako and Zach would use their full speed to outdo the other.

It wasn't all sword fighting though. There were the sessions where Mako had his student stand in front an archery target; Mako would stand twenty meters away equipped with a longbow, firing arrow after arrow.

With the arrows flying and heading straight at him, Zach's job was to catch them, to take his position and stand perfectly relaxed. When the arrows were just a fraction of a second, away from piercing his flesh, almost all of the young boy's body would remain completely still, as his trusty right hand did all the work, whizzing through almost frozen time to catch the arrows. Throughout the entire training session, not once did Zach fail to catch a single arrow.

Mako had Zach do laps around the island, both running and swimming. To begin with, Zach would have to do the swimming alone, but during the last week, Mako had joined his young companion in the water and challenged him to races. The first two days saw Zach as the victor.

To make it more difficult, Mako changed the races completely. For the rest of the week, Zach had to race swimming underwater. Every time he had to surface for air, he had to stop, giving Mako a time advantage.

The first two revised races saw Mako win with Zach trailing behind him, but the more they raced, the faster the young boy from Mantos became and his breath-holds lasted much longer, enabling him to start winning the races once again.

It wasn't all just swimming, arrow catching, running and sword fighting though; during the two weeks of training, Mako took the time to teach Zach about other weapons and had him use them, having him engage in combat armed with a spear, a lance, even a battle axe. Although Zach possessed great skill with them, he much preferred to fight with a sword.

Another training tactic that Mako had Zach do was to hang off the edge of the volcano and have him hold on for as long as he could before pulling himself up. Letting go was not an option because if Zach let go, he will surely fall to his death.

To start with, the muscle pain was Zach's biggest problem. His muscles screamed out in agony but as he learned endurance, his muscles got used to it, and the muscle pain faded to the point where Zach hardly noticed it anymore.

No longer bothered by the muscle aches, he started to get bored instead, so to keep himself entertained he began doing pull-ups, pulling himself up and then lowering himself back down while clinging to the edge. Mako would stand by, watching over him, ready to act if need be.

Mako was very pleased with Zach's progress. His speed and strength had grown almost to the point where he was equal with Mako in the Blood Rush. In some aspects, Zach was much better, just a little faster when it came to battling and he was more cunning.

Mako was still able to hold his own, his vast knowledge and experience serving him well.

Just like every day for the last two weeks, Zach was training once again, this time at the beach in the rough water, as droplets of rain fell down from the dull grey sky. Mako was standing on the sandy part of the beach, watching his student battle against the waves.

"Keep going; you're almost done!" the master swordsman instructed, watching his disciple tread water.

"How long have I been doing this?" Zach asked, doing breaststrokes to remain afloat. A wave hit him in the face and made him swallow a mouthful of salt water. Zach coughed and sputtered as he attempted to clear his airways.

"Keep your mouth shut!" Mako commanded.

Zach obeyed and nodded. He decided to communicate telepathically, and reflected that when he first told Mako he could do this, his teacher acted surprised.

*Seriously though, how much longer?*

*Mere minutes.* Mako replied. *How are you handling the weight?*

The weight Mako referred to was an iron shield that weighed a solid seventy pounds. Zach was holding onto it with his legs, the shield trying to pull him down.

*Okay, seeing as how it is heavier than the last one,* Zach joked in reply. The last one was another iron shield that only weighed forty pounds.

Mako let Zach's attempt at humor slide, not bothering to dignify it with a response. Instead, he let Zach continue to support himself for another ten minutes before calling time.

"Okay, come on back!" Mako called.

"I'm coming!" Zach yelled, and swam easily back to the shore.

"I brought you a souvenir," Zach joked, wearing a cheeky grin, as he exhibited the shield to Mako.

"So I see," Mako retorted, extracting his long sword and then bent over to scoop up Zach's sword from a boulder to his left. "You'll want this," he commented, tossing it to Zach, who tied it on his belt.

"Yes, Zach, you will want to pull it free, but first..." The reason for the pause in speech was because Mako wanted to pull out the brown cloth he had tucked away around his belt and holds it up for Zach to see. "...you need to put your blindfold on."

Zach smiled.

Mako took the cloth from his belt and tied it around Zach's head, careful not to leave any gaps.

"Can you see anything?" Mako asked.

"No, nothing," Zach replied truthfully.

"Good, now draw your weapon," Mako commanded, holding his own sword, gripping it with both hands, keeping it close to his body.

Obeying his tutor's order and acting instinctively, Zach's right hand flew to his sword hilt, readying himself for combat.

"Now remember, a good swordsman is the master of their sword, but a great swordsman is the master of their enemies," the older Watcher said, recalling one of his more favorite quotes. "Now are you ready?"

"I'm ready," the young Watcher replied just before Mako lashed out with a horizontal slash, which Zach countered easily.

Mako drew back and lunged forward, only to have Zach side step the move and leap on top of a large slanted rock, off to his right.

"Very good, now keep it going," The older swordsman ordered before he proceeds with his onslaught of attacks. He charged at his young student and let loose a volley of swings, the steel blade cutting through both air and rain, but not Zach, who, even with a blindfold on, was able to protect himself as he used his own sword to ward off Mako's attacks.

"Very good," Mako commented, approving of how well Zach was doing.

A smile of satisfaction crossed Zach's face. He was able to predict Mako's attacks. All thanks to the blindfold training, Zach's sensory ability was able to grow and grow.

However, he could no longer see like he did earlier

on when he was in the boat cave and saw Izal in his mind.

As Mako was about to strike once again, Zach felt a new presence homing in on their position.

"Wait! I feel something." the boy declared as he removed his blindfold.

"What is it?" Mako said, silently praying that Shimay hadn't broken out of the temple just yet.

"Izal! It's Izal!" The Apprentice Watcher replied excitedly, feeling the raven draw nearer.

"Are you sure?" Mako asked, watching the skies.

"Positive," Zach responded, as both he and Mako sheathed their weapons.

"You're sure it's not Shimay?" Mako interjected.

"I'm positive. Plus, Shimay wouldn't approach us from the water, would he?"

"No, he wouldn't."

"And not only can I feel him, I can see him," Zach confessed. Off in the distance he could just see the raven flying toward them.

*Caw!*

*Hello boys, did you miss me?* Izal's voice boomed inside their heads. *Meet me up at the house we need to talk!* The raven soared over them. They immediately gave chase, eager to hear Izal's news.

# CHAPTER XXIV:

## *Some Troubling News*

Flames of orange, yellow and red burned brightly, bringing light and warmth to the room. Having changed clothes, they all enjoyed the heat from a roaring fire.

"Tell me, old friend, did you find what we seek?" Mako inquired.

*Sadly no.* Izal replies from his stool by the table. Zach had prepared a meal for him containing some cooked vegetables and day-old bread.

"Then why have you returned? I thought I told you stay away until you were able to find a solution to ending Zach's memory loss."

*I know that, but sadly, there is no spell or enchantment that can help us. All I was able to gather was a couple of theories.*

"Well, that's better than nothing." Zach commented.

*Thank you, Zach.*

"So what are these theories then?" Mako probed.

*The first theory I got is from a friend of mine on Retina. He believes Zach's memory may return if Shimay is destroyed. Another is that it will return naturally over time. The third one is about taking him to an Indiunia priestess and have her do a recovery enchantment.*

"Which I've already told you is impossible. We don't have one and there is no way I can just take Zach to Indiania, what with it crawling with Shanzi. Do you have another other theories?"

*"Just one; however, I believe it is our best and only option."*

"Which is?" Zach asked.

*A Shanzi warlock can easily restore Zach's memories.*

"What's a Shanzi warlock?" Zach asked. Until now, he had never heard the term before.

*A Shanzi warlock is like any other type of Shanzi. They come in many forms, except instead of just possessing powers best suited to their habitat, personality, form, classification and breed of Dark Ones, Shanzi warlocks also possess the gift of magic, able to conjure magical elemental attacks and they have been known to be masters of memory, able to erase your every thought and create memory blocks.*

"Where can we find one?" Zach asked.

"Indiania is full of Shanzi, so there's a good chance you can find one there," Mako frowned.

"Then that's where we go!" Zach exclaimed.

"No, Zach, no one is going anywhere. We can't risk leaving, not when Shimay could break free any day now!" Mako's mighty voice boomed as he expressed his displeasure.

"But..." Zach began to argue.

"But nothing! No one is leaving, especially for Indiania."

*Actually, I was thinking more of the Mares Realm itself. After all, at one time, it was the home of a renowned Shanzi warlock, who served under the one and only Lord Darkari,* Izal said.

"You're referring to Gremora, aren't you?" Mako asked.

*You are correct, and as you know, neither you nor Iris were able to vanquish him and there is no known record of his destruction.*

"I highly doubt he is still alive, not after all of these years."

*I beg to differ, old man,* Izal retorted.

"And what? You believe him to still be around,

154

hiding like a rat on one of the unpopulated islands?"

*He could be!* Izal replied.

"You would like to go off and look for him, would you?"

*If Gremora could free Zach's memories, then yes, I do!*

"I'm sorry, Izal, but I cannot allow that," the Guardian of Iris snapped.

"Why not?" Zach asked.

"Because Gremora is Shanzi, our sworn enemy. Why the hell would he help us? Also, going off to track down a Dark One that may or may not still be alive would take a lot of time, time that would be better spent getting Zach ready for Shimay."

*Fine then, but there is one more thing,* Izal replied.

"And what's that?" Mako gazed intently at the raven.

*The island east of here, Osiris Island..."* Izal began.

"What about Osiris?" Zach questioned. If travelling by Delfini, was only around half a day to a full day's sail away, depending on wind conditions.

*There's a goblin camp set up in the Osiris Ruins,* Izal said.

The Osiris Ruins used to be the Osiris Palace, the holiday home of the Mares royal family. During the long years of war, the palace was destroyed and the royal family never bothered to have it rebuilt.

"And your point is?" Mako asked.

*It's goblins.* Izal answered. *A tribe of them.*

"So you'd like us to do what? Go in there and take them out? Goblins are the least of our worries at the moment." Mako's eyes hardened

*You do not understand!*

"Then make me understand!"

*There are a vast number of goblins in the camp; at least forty of them and they are heavily armed. If they were*

155

*to reach any populated island, without a Watcher or regiment of Royal Guard, they would easily overrun it.*

"That's terrible!" Zach exclaimed in shock. "We must do something."

"And we will, but after we have dealt with Shimay!" Mako's replied hotly.

*There are children, Mako, locked in steel cages, being treated like wild animals.* Izal divulged.

"What did you say?" He asked with disbelief, as he, like Zach, stood up.

*The goblins have children held prisoner and I didn't get a great look, but I would say that some have been there for years, raised in captivity.*

Both Zach and Mako were speechless and disgusted at the same time. Mako felt especially bad—if there really was a goblin camp with children prisoners then he should have known about it, should have done something about it.

"You say you believe some have been there for years?" Mako asked.

*Yes,* Izal nodded sadly.

"Is it possible that some or all of them have been there since they were babies?" Zach asked.

*It is possible, yes.* Izal replied.

"Then is it possible that some of those children that you've spoken about, could have been sent here only to wind up at Osiris instead, and have been taken captive by the goblins?"

And there it was. Mako had asked the crucial question he was putting off.

*It is highly possible, yes. After all, thirty-one years have passed and the only boy to wash up on our beach isn't even from this realm. The population of the Mares Realm has been on the rise the last few decades. In short, yes, it makes perfect sense that your potential students washed up on the wrong island.*

"Then we must go get them. Take out every single

goblin and rescue those children!" Zach cried.

"And what if I say no? What if I forbid you to go?" Mako asked.

"I'd go anyway!" Zach declared, locking eyes with his mentor.

"Why? Why put your life at risk? Why risk your life for children you don't even know?"

"Because it is the right thing to do! It is what we do and what you've spent all these years trying to teach me." Zach replied, refusing to back down. "Because this is what you've been training me for my whole life."

"What I have been training you for these last two weeks is to defeat Shimay." Mako countered, secretly pleased with what Zach was saying.

"And I will, but we need to go to Osiris, we need to free those kids." Zach pleaded.

"Tell me, Zach, the moment my back is turned, you are not going to go sneaking off on one of my boats and sail off to Osiris and take on those goblins are you?"

"Actually, that is exactly what I am going to do," Zach confessed.

"You'd go in there, all on your own?" Mako probed.

"Yes, I would. I'm a Watcher and it's what we do," Zach boasted proudly, maintaining his intensive gaze. Mako began to smile.

"Yes, you are a Watcher, you are determined to do the right thing, no matter what and for that I am pleased, but I can't let you risk your life on such a mission with Shimay on the loose," Mako replied, hoping that Zach would understand.

Placing his right hand on top of Mako's left, Zach gazed into his eyes. "Master, I can do this!"

"I know you can, Zach, but you need to finish your training."

*If you truly desire Zach to get stronger, to be ready for Shimay, then you would be wise to let him go.*

Mako turned to Izal, his eyes burning intensely. "Explain."

*Zach could have all the training in the world and yes, he would be strong for it, but if you let him undergo this mission, not only will he be strong for it, but wise too.*

"You're talking about experience," Mako replied with a nod.

*Battle experience to be precise, but yes.*

"You make an excellent point and I can't really believe that I'm going to say this, but, Zach..." Mako looked at his student. "...you best get an early night, you leave for Osiris in the morning."

A huge smile flashed across Zach's face, and he tore up the stairs to his room. Mako looked at Izal. "Are you happy now?"

# CHAPTER XXV:

## *Setting Sail at Sunrise*

During the long cold night that passed, Zach's dreams ran wild. He dreamed of a tall man, muscular and well-toned. The man wore a black tunic, with a silver breastplate and silver shoulder pads. His sleeves and leggings were dark grey. He wore black fingerless gloves and leather boots. His face was rugged but youthful, his blue eyes sharp but kind. His blond hair was plentiful and he was armed with a long sword much like Mako's, the weapon baring the mark of a Watcher.

He was running through a forest of trees unfamiliar to Zach; his boots crushing the leaves beneath his feet. He broke through the woods to a clearing, and ran along the edge of a sharp cliff where a vast gushing waterfall spilled down to the bottom.

Suddenly the man heard shrieks and movement behind him; the creatures he was running from had caught up. In a fight, he could easily take them all on, but now was the time for flight, not fight.

"Prepare to die, Watcher!" A gruff, ferocious voice boomed from amongst the trees, the mysterious voice speaking in the Algean language.

"Never say die!" the Watcher remarked playfully, just before he leaped off the cliff.

A huge six-meter tall ogre burst out of the trees, scanning the cliff face for the jumper, who sliced through the surface of the water below, just as Zach burst awake, panting loudly.

*That dream, I've had it before.*

Before he could decide what to do, his bedroom door opened and Mako walked in, with a lit lantern in hand.

"Oh good, you're up," Mako commented. "Get dressed, it's time to go."

"I'll be right out," Zach said, hurriedly dressing and tying his sword to his belt.

When he got downstairs, he noticed that the fire from the night before was still burning and Mako and Izal were eating breakfast.

"Come get something to eat," Mako said, beckoning Zach to the table.

*Morning, Zach.* Izal greeted.

"Morning," Zach said, taking a seat. He was greeted by a huge bowl full of soup, but as he ran his spoon through the thick brown liquid, he noticed chunks of chicken amongst potatoes, carrots, and mushrooms.

"When did we get chicken again?" Zach asked, reaching for the bread-stick.

"A passing cargo ship made a delivery of food while you were busy yesterday morning during your meditation training." Mako answered.

Cargo ships brought most of their supplies. Anything from food, livestock, and various other necessities came to them regularly and at no cost. For Mares Law declared all materials and foods required by the Guardians and students of the Isle of Iris were given freely in exchange for their services.

"Now I put a whole chicken into your soup, so make sure you eat up. You'll need the energy."

"You want me to eat all of this?" Zach looked skeptically at his bowl. There was easily enough food in it for two adults, far too much for his small stomach.

"And the bread too," Mako added.

Zach rolled his eyes. He could easily hang on the edge of a volcano for hours, but eating all this food was the real challenge.

It took him a full twenty minutes to eat everything. When he was finally finished, he aided Mako in filling up two bottles with drinking water, and filling a couple of large jars with the rich soup broth.

With the supplies bottled, they wrapped them up in a large cloth and loaded it into a big wicker basket. They also put in a couple of bowls, spoons, and an iron pan for cooking.

Zach and Mako took turns carrying the basket down the volcano to the shore, each carrying a lit lantern, as Izal flew overhead. The moon was bright and the island bathed in moonlight.

In the water, sitting five meters off shore was one of Mako's Delfinis, currently anchored up.

"You got the Delfini out all by yourself?" Zach asked.

"The one you're thinking about is still on its stand in the boat cave. This is the other one, the one I keep in the sea cavern."

The sea cavern that Mako mentioned was a large cavern that ran right under the island from the southernmost point to the island's westernmost point. Most of it was wide enough for a small boat to get through. It allowed him to move his boats away from the open sea and hide them under the island, where they could be safeguarded. But it wasn't all just waterways. One part of the cavern led above ground via a passage connected to the boat cave. It had a slipway to help get the boats into the water quicker.

"When did you bring it round?" Zach asked.

"This morning while you were still asleep. Now listen up. There is plenty of food, but while sailing, eat only the bread, you can have some of the soup cold, but bread will be better. Now, you have sailed a Delfini around Iris, but you've never sailed away to foreign lands, so you may get a little seasick. When you land on Osiris, you can eat as much hot soup as you want. Provided you hide yourself in one of its caves and light your fire there, where it will not be seen. You should be able to take a nap in there as well, but make sure you stay alert; goblins have a habit of sneaking up on people when their backs are turned."

"Eat bread when sailing, eat hot soup on land, but only if sheltered in a cave and if I have to sleep, do it in the cave, but stay alert because goblins are sneaky," the young Watcher reiterated.

"Good. On the western side of the island, which is the side you are to sail to, is a sea cave, which you can sail into and hide your boat in. Do you understand?"

"I understand," Zach said.

"You do not have to do this if you don't want to; you can still walk away." Mako said, giving Zach one last opportunity to back down.

"I want to do this!" Zach replied with a reassuring grin. "Anything else I need to know?"

"There will be a slight storm today, mostly wind, but it will be coming from the east blowing west and instead of struggling to sail through it, I'd prefer it if you rowed. It's good training that way."

"I'll keep that in mind."

"And remember, you are there on a rescue mission. Your sole goal is to save the children, nothing else." Mako pointed a finger at Zach as if he were cross with him. "You are not there to kill all the goblins—only, and I mean *only*, engage them in battle if you have no other choice. We can always deal with them another time."

"As you wish, Master." Zach bowed courteously.

"Good, now what are you there for?"

"A rescue mission."

"And what are you not there for?" Mako probed, lowering his finger.

"I'm not there to slay the goblins."

"Attaboy. Now let us get you aboard that boat."

As Zach climbed aboard, Mako lifted the wicker basket into the boat. Izal sat idly by, as he watched night fade; sunrise had begun.

"But, Zach, do not engage in battle..." Mako began to repeat his previous warning, standing waist high in the water, only to be interrupted by Zach, who grasped two oars, ready to start rowing.

"Unless I have no other choice," he finished.

"One last thing," Mako said. "Goblins are both cunning and ruthless. If in a fight, they will not fight fair, or hold back, so neither should you. You are both faster and stronger than they are, therefore you have the advantage."

"I won't hold back," Zach solemnly swore.

Even though Zach has already made his oath, Mako still felt the urge to push his point. "I mean it, Zach, if you do find yourself having to fight, draw your sword and start swinging and do not stop until you are the last one standing."

"I swear," Zach replied. Mako gave the boat a slight push toward the open sea.

"Good luck!" he called out, retrieving his lantern.

*Caw!*

*Good luck, Zach!* Izal cried out.

"Bye!" Zach called back, waving briefly and extinguished his lantern, rowing toward the rising sun.

Standing on the mostly stony beach, both Izal and Mako watched Zach as he rowed away, getting smaller and smaller as the sun rose higher and higher.

Mako turned to Izal, something clearly on his mind.

*What is it, Mako?* Izal asked.

"I want you to go with him."

*Why? Zach can do this alone.*

"I know he can, but given the current situation, I would very much like it if you went with him," Mako said. "You know the island, you know the ruins, so you'd be perfect to advise him."

*I could go with him, yes, and I would be an asset, but you need me here for when Shimay escapes. I'm the one who can sense him, not you.*

"Izal, it is because of you that Zach is sailing off to an island overrun with goblins and even though I would much prefer it if he didn't fight, I know that he will. I need you to keep an eye on him, keep him safe. Please?"

*All right,* Izal said, for he too was worried about Zach.

*Thank you, my friend, and good luck.*

*And to you.*

# CHAPTER XXVI:

## *The Voyage to Osiris*

**Z**ach wasn't all too happy to have Izal join him on his first ever quest. He believed it to be a sign that Mako didn't believe that he was capable of completing his task all on his own, but as his journey from Iris to Osiris progressed, he began to feel grateful for the company.

Since he set out and started rowing, a full fourteen hours have passed; the sun has risen and set as day had come and gone. Once again, night reigned supreme and the moon, one day away from being full, occupied the sky.

During the past fourteen hours, Zach had rowed and rowed, battling against the wind that blew from the east. At last, the wind changed direction. With a gentle breeze coming from the southwest, Zach deployed the sails and used the wind to push his vessel onward.

Crouched down to keep himself warm, with the oars laying beneath the seats, Zach chewed on a bread stick. The lantern sat at his feet, lit against the cloudy sky.

Zach looked up and saw Izal perched on the bow.

*Hey, Izal!* Zach called out in thought.

*Yes, Zach?*

*I know this might not be the best time to bring this up, but I had that dream again.*

*The dream?* Izal let his mind drift back to a time when Zach was younger and dreamed of the mysterious man, on the run from an ogre.

*The dream with the man?*

*Yes.*

*That is most unusual.*

*And it's got me thinking.*

*About?*

*His voice, it's so familiar, I think I've heard it somewhere before...*

*Zach.* Izal interrupted.

*And he looks familiar too, I think I might even know him.*

*I highly doubt that. Mako is the only adult you have ever met, besides Shimay.*

"Well, what about my father? Surely back when I was a baby I would've heard his voice and seen his face?" Zach wondered aloud. "Isn't it possible that the man in the dream could be my father? After all, the man looks a lot like me, just older."

*That man is not your father, Zach.* Izal said.

"Well, why not?" Zach protested loudly, taking his hand away from the rudder and snuffing the lantern.

*Because as you have mentioned to me before, the man in your dream is a Watcher and as you know, Watchers are forbidden to marry and have children. Having loved ones is a distraction. A Watcher's priority is everyone comes first, not your loved ones first and everyone else second.*

"I know that, but..."

*But nothing, Zach. I don't know who the man in your dream is, but whoever it is, he is not your father, you can take my word for that.*

"Fine," Zach wasn't particularly happy with Izal's tone.

*Besides, it is more likely you are dreaming of a future event.*

"And why would I dream of a future event?"

*Why would you dream of a father you don't know?* Izal countered.

"I can't be dreaming of the future because if you're right, then that would mean that the man in the dream..."

*Is you,* Izal answered.

"But that doesn't make any sense," Zach replied.

*Actually, it makes perfect sense,* Izal retorted. *After all, it is you who said that the man looks like you, and it was you who says his voice is familiar too, maybe because it is you that you are dreaming of.*

"I guess," Zach admitted.

*Now, let us say no more on this subject and focus more on the task at hand.*

"And that is?"

*There is another reason why I wanted you to go to Osiris and it is a reason Mako cannot know.*

"And that is?"

*There is a power level on the island, much stronger than the goblins. It might be an ogre or something even stronger, but regardless of what it is, if you were to destroy it, you will become even stronger, stronger than Shimay.*

"How strong is it?"

*Honestly, it's a lot more powerful then you are now, but I have faith in you and your skills. Regardless of how strong it is, I know in my heart you will prevail.*

"You truly believe I can beat this unknown force?" Zach asked.

*Yes.*

"Then I'll do it, especially if it will help me destroy Shimay. Seeing as how it is my fault he got to be so strong," he declared, ready and willing for a fight.

*Good. Now, with your ability, you should be able to sense everyone on the island   human, goblin and whatever else is there, so trust your senses, they can and will warn you of approaching enemies.*

"Right."

*Also, because I know you will notice it once we reach shore, it's best I come clean. There aren't around forty goblins, but more like sixty. I'm not sure, I couldn't get an accurate reading and not all of them are your usual normal goblins, but...*

"But what?"

*They're Wikita goblins, from the Indiania Realm.* Izal replied.

"Wikita goblins, as in the ones who grow to be as big as humans? Are red and brown in color and immune to most magic? And are faster and stronger than most?" Zach asked, recalling from his studies.

*Yes, Zach, Wikita goblins. There are also Forest goblins there too, which as you know are smaller, slower, weaker, and stupid.*

"You're lucky Mako doesn't know about this."

*Maybe, but you're veering off course. Turn to starboard.*

Zach adjusted the ship's heading. "So where are the children being kept?"

*They are being contained in metal cages in the courtyard of the palace and in order to reach them, you'll need to get past the outer perimeter wall, which is guarded by patrols of goblins.*

"I could just go on an all-out offensive, but that wouldn't work, if my presence is discovered, then they'll just seal the gates, preventing me from getting in."

*Not really, with your climbing skills I bet you could easily climb over the wall or I could simplify matters and fly you in.*

"That would get me in, but I need to get into the courtyard unnoticed and marching through a ruined palace full of goblins isn't exactly the easiest thing to do. No, I need a clever way to get in."

*A plan will come to you, I'm sure of it.* Izal replied.

Zach raised his head and looked to the night sky. The bright stars brought him inspiration, blessing him with a sure-fire plan.

*You've got an idea, haven't you?* Izal asked, feeling it swirling around inside Zach's head.

"Yes, I have." His blue eyes were lit up with

excitement.

*And judging by that look in your eyes, I'd say it's a good one.*

"No, it's a *great* one," retorted the boy. "But I will require some assistance that only you can give me."

*What will I have to do?* questioned the raven.

"I'll tell you when we land, but first I'm going to get us some help," he replied, leaning over one side of the boat and looking into the water. Closing his eyes, he let his ability take over and was overwhelmed by all the life forces around him.

*What do you mean help?*

"Dolphins. There is a pod of them about a hundred meters off our stern and I'm going to get them to give us a hand."

*And how are you going to do that?* Izal inquired.

"I'm going to save a dolphin from a shark." Before Izal could even make a reply, Zach dived into the cold sea.

*Zach! Zach, get back here!*

Zach ignored him, going deep. It was not long before he spotted a great white shark in pursuit of a bottlenose dolphin.

The shark made repeated attempts to catch the dolphin's tail, but after repeated failures, it resorted to its last tactic. It dove down and ahead of its prey, it planned its ambush.

Watching the shark, Zach knew that this time the dolphin could not escape. Gathering all his strength and speed, he rammed the shark, punching it in the nose.

The bottlenose pivoted and looked down, disbelievingly.

*Get out of here now!* Zach shouted at it.

Instead of obeying Zach, the dolphin chose to stay and fight. Just as the shark went to charge at Zach, the dolphin rammed it, allowing Zach to punch it in the nose again. Dazed, the shark hovered in the water, unsure of what hit it. Zach caught its dorsal fin with one hand and pulled his sword free with the other.

Plunging his sword into the shark's brain, he quickly pulled it free, engulfed in a cloud of blood before he made his move toward the surface.

*That was close. Air. I need air.*

As if hearing him, the dolphin nudged him. Zach grabbed hold of its dorsal fin, and was gulping in fresh air in seconds.

"Thank you," Zach said, before he climbed into the boat and leaned over the side. Izal was outraged.

The dolphin grinned at him and started to chatter. Zach decided to establish a mind link with it.

*No, thank you. That shark had been trailing us for weeks and now we are free. I am in your debt,* the dolphin clicked.

*I don't need anyone in my debt, but I'd gladly accept a friend,* Zach smiled.

*I would be most glad to be your friend. I am Fluke, a member of the Mares pod.* Fluke replied.

*Pleased to meet you, Fluke. I am Zach of Iris, a student of Mako, and I am on a mission to reach Osiris. There are children in need of saving.*

*You are on a quest to save others and yet you helped me anyway. For that, I am your friend for life, Zach of Iris, and am at your service whenever you need me, starting now,* the joyous Fluke replied, whistling to signal his pod to come to him.

*Zach, what the hell is going on?* Izal asked, noticing the approaching thirty dolphins.

*We will have you at Osiris in no time at all,* Fluke announced to a satisfied Zach. Satisfied for two reasons: he'd made a new friend for life and his plan had worked.

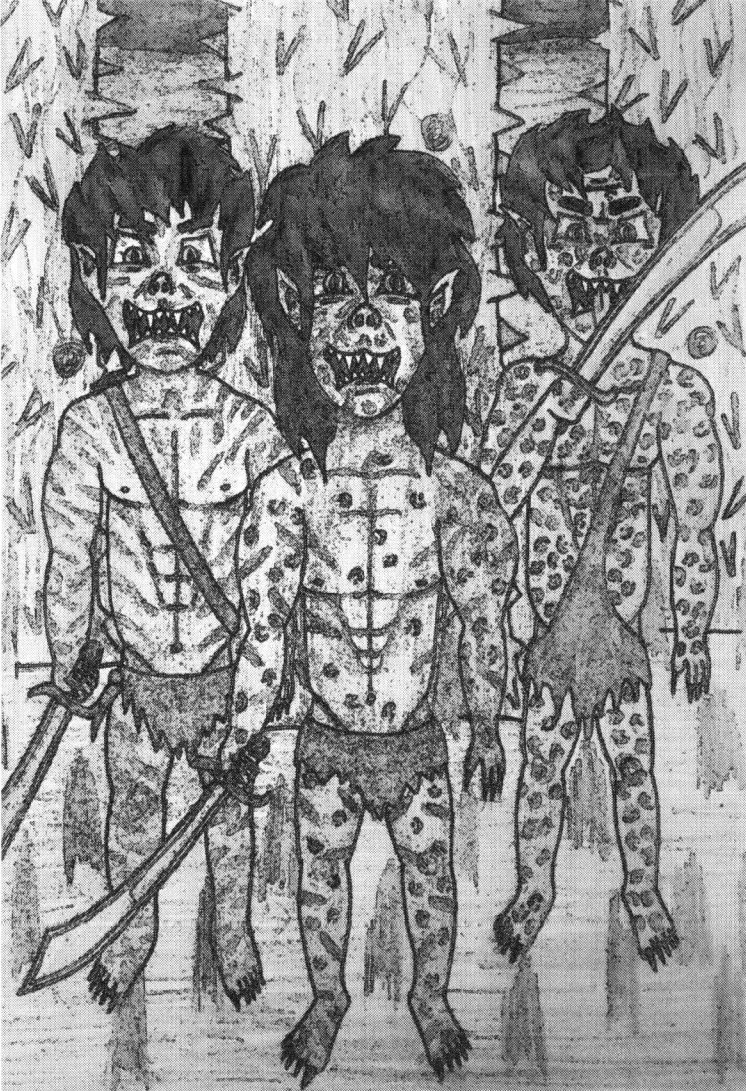

# CHAPTER XXVII:

## *The Ruins of Osiris*

With the help of the dolphins, which Zach had tied several lengths of rope to, the Delfini was towed to Osiris very quickly, arriving at the island four hours before sunrise.

Upon his arrival at the triangularly shaped island, Zach easily found the sea cave on the western side. The moon illuminated the entrance and, with the help of the dolphins, he was able to navigate the vessel deep into the cave, and anchor it to nearby stalagmites.

All but one of the dolphins left, leaving Zach, Izal, and Fluke behind in the sea cave. Fluke drifted around the boat, while Izal stood on the cold, hard rock floor, looking down toward the tunnel opening. The young Watcher was lying under the seats of the Delfini, with the folded up sails wrapped around him like a quilt.

Zach slept peacefully for six hours, awaking fully refreshed. He asked Izal to fetch some twigs and leaves so he could build a fire. In the meantime, he explored a bit and discovered that the tunnel that brought them in went to the surface, into a small forest.

As they waited for the raven to return, Zach spent the time getting to know more about his new dolphin friend, learning of how the great white shark had been trailing the pod of dolphins for the last four weeks. He also learned that the Watchers were still well known, not just by humans, elves, ogres and Shanzi, but also to every race, every animal and insect, as is the eternal conflict with the Dark Ones.

When Izal returned, he brought with him many thin branches with plenty of leaves on them, so Zach ripped the leaves off and chopped up the branches.

In no time at all, Zach had a good fire going, and heated up some soup, as his companions watched with interest.

*Hey, Izal.*

*Yes, Zach.*

*Would you like anything to eat? Bread? Soup?* Zach offered kindly.

*Thank you, but I'm fine. I had some worms when I was out gathering materials for the fire.*

"Suit yourself." Zach said before taking another bite of bread. *What about you, Fluke? Would you like some bread?*

*That food is for you and the children; it is not for feeding overgrown fish,* Izal protested with disgust.

"Firstly, Izal, dolphins are mammals, not fish, and secondly, Fluke is my friend, he has aided us. Offering him something to eat is the least we can do." *Fluke, would you like something to eat?*

*Best not, Izal doesn't look too happy. Besides, I can easily catch some fish so I'll be fine.* Fluke replied graciously, diving and heading out to sea.

"See what you've done, you've made him leave," Zach scowled.

*Good riddance if you ask me. Now eat up, we've got a rescue mission to be getting on with!* The raven snapped, flying off.

Twenty minutes passed. Zach finished eating, cleaned and repacked his supplies and put the basket back in the boat. Now ready to venture out and get on with the task, Zach put one foot in front of the other and left the chamber, headed for the forest.

Emerging from the tunnel, he was momentarily blinded. As soon as his vision returned, he spotted the raven perched on a nearby branch.

*Are you sure you want to go through with this? We*

*could always think of another plan if you want to.* Izal called out to him.

"My plan is the best one we have and I know it will work," Zach replied as he undid his sheath from his belt and held it out for Izal to take.

"Now hold onto this for me and make sure you stay out of sight. Remain in the cave if you have to, but remember to listen out for my thoughts. I will call your name three times and when you hear them, that is your cue to home in on my position."

*As you wish.* Izal took flight, leaving Zach in the forest.

*Well, I guess I best get on with it.* he thought to himself.

He kept his speed nice and slow so he could easily be discovered by the goblins.

Staying inside the forest, Zach avoided the ruins. He suddenly felt eight life forces nearby and closing in on him, so he decided to make things even easier for the goblins and began shouting, charging toward them.

"Help! Help!" he yelled in the Wikita language, running as if something were chasing him, right in front of a Wikitan goblin patrol.

Zach stopped dead, taking in every detail. The eight goblins were exactly as they had been described to him. Each one had long, pointed ears, monstrous eyes, mouths full of razor sharp teeth capable of biting through bone and pig like snouts for noses. Each wore a dirty loincloth and all similarly armed with a falchion. Zach noted that all of them had yellow eyes save for the lead one, whose eyes were green.

Gulping in fear, Zach stood transfixed, his eyes widening in terror. All of them look ready to cut him into pieces.

"Get him!" the lead goblin roared, drawing his own weapons: a single-edged curved sword and an axe.

Seven of the eight Wikita goblins charged at Zach, who turned and ran as fast as he could without going into the Blood Rush.

He could feel their heavy breathing behind him and hear their every step and started to wish that he had his sword with him, even a wooden one. But he knew it had to be like this; otherwise his plan would not work.

"Get him!" the lead goblin shouted again, as he too gave chase and caught up with the others.

"Yes, sir!" the other goblins cried out in unison, maintaining their pursuit.

Zach decided it was time to stop running around in circles and head for the ruins. The patrol followed him, happy he was going where they wanted him to on his own.

Standing on top of the hill was what was left of the four hundred year old palace. While much broken down, the palace still had a high stone perimeter wall. Of greater interest were all the goblins posted along it, many armed with bows. One of them saw him.

"*Intruder!*" Zach ducked quickly to avoid the arrow. He heard a horn being blown, and saw masses of goblins swarming toward him.

"*Archers fire!*" a loud, shrill voice called out. The order to attack came from another green-eyed goblin.

Forty arrows shot into the air and began to fall. Zach was just able to dodge each one. The goblins giving chase, however, were not as fortunate as they got struck down by their fellows.

"Hold your fire!" a new voice ordered. This voice, which also spoke in the Wikita tongue, was more human; commanding, powerful and higher pitched.

Zach looked up to see who it was. About the same height as the goblins, the owner of the voice was dressed in a full suit of armor of silver and gold. Zach recognized it to be of Indianian make; armor, which had blessed with magical enchantments that made it weightless and impenetrable.

The man in the armor, armed with a sword in a gold sheath strapped to his back, pulled free his shining blade and shoved a goblin out of his way before leaping off the wall.

So far, the goblins were playing right into his hands, even if there were more of them than he had originally thought.

The armored man landed silently behind Zach on the bright green grass. He struck the Watcher in the back of the head, sending him crashing face first to the grass, where he feigned unconsciousness.

With his prey out for the count, Zach's attacker removed the golden helmet. Shaking loose her hair, the pretty, thirteen year old turned her brilliant blue eyes to the goblins nearest her. Zach's attacker was a very attractive young girl with defined check-bones, a small chin, long, golden, wavy hair, and noticeable blue eyes.

"Throw him in a cage with the others. He should make a fine meal for our king!" she ordered. The goblins rushed to do her bidding.

# CHAPTER XXVIII:

## *Lagos and Jasmine*

Within seconds of being hit on the head, Zach lay limply in his captors' hands as they picked him up and carried him beyond the perimeter wall and into the courtyard. He carefully opened one eye just a fraction to observe what he could. Then he was chucked into a large metal cage already home to three occupants.

For good measure, Zach choose to spend the next half hour lying motionless inside the cage, playing his unconscious card a little longer, keeping his eyes shut and his mind focused on using his abilities to get a more accurate figure of just how many creatures inhabited the island.

Dividing them into their different classifications, he is able to determine that there were fifty-two Wikita goblins, twenty-nine scrawny Forest goblins, also called Fori, one large life force that he couldn't pin down, and nine humans, including the girl who struck him. One of the humans was fading fast.

Zach was intrigued by her level of power. She was physically strong, but most of her strength came from the magic she bore.

He also found Izal, still safe in the cave, and breathed an inner sigh of relief.

Zach couldn't help but think about the lovely girl who attacked him. He hadn't seen a female before, but more than that, he felt drawn to her, as if they shared the same important destiny.

Tired of feigning unconsciousness, Zach opened his eyes and stood up inside the cast iron cage. It was four meters long and two meters high. He looked around the courtyard, seeing two other cages of the same size, both holding the children Izal had mentioned. In the first cage, he saw two older boys with their hands on their ears and eyes closed, as if trying to shut off the outside world, while in the other cage, three young boys were huddled together.

Moving his gaze away from the cages, Zach spotted a regiment of twenty goblins and a small squad of archers up on the outer wall. The rest had disappeared. He hoped they'd gone someplace distant; there wouldn't be so many to fight. He already knew where they were, but he wanted to see how they were armed. Just before they noticed him looking at them, he quickly turned away to see who shared the cage with him.

A young brown haired boy around four years old looked at Zach with brown eyes full of fear. The second boy, slightly younger than Zach, looked warily at him. Both boys were dirty and reeked to high heaven. They were barefoot and wore filthy, torn sheepskin clothing.

The third occupant looked to be in his sixties. His face was old and wrinkled, and sported a long, pointed white beard and wild hair that fell to his waist. Unlike the two boys, his green eyes showed no fear, only acceptance and kindness. He dressed much like Mako.

*Can I help you?* Zach questioned telepathically.

"I...I can hear you, in my head," the man stammered, in the language of the goblins.

"Ah, Wikita, I speak it," Zach replied

"Who are you?"

*Well, Lagos, I'm Zach,* he said, using the name he read in the man's mind.

*You know my name?*

*Yes, I do,* he confirmed with a friendly smile, as he projected his voice into Lagos' head once again.

*And I can read your mind, which is exactly where I would prefer to have our conversation. This way no one can overhear us.*

*You're a Watcher, aren't you?* Lagos looked down at the boys. "Lay down, children, get some rest." They nodded, found a corner, and curled up to sleep.

*Technically, I'm a Watcher's apprentice, whereas you are a full-fledged Watcher, aren't you?*

*Yes, I am,* Lagos answered.

*From the Indiania Realm, obviously, but which island?*

*Celestrial.*

The moment Zach heard Celestrial his mind began to race. Celestrial was the capital of Indiania, the largest island in the realm and home to the royal family of Indiania, rulers of the realm and servants to the divine Wikita priestesses. Chosen girls blessed with unique magical powers.

*You're a long way away from Celestrial. What brings you to this side of the world?*

*What brings you here?* Lagos quizzed in return.

*You didn't answer my question, which indicates you mean to hide something from me, which is pointless. Yes, you are very sick and your days in this world are close to their end, but your secrets will not die with you. If I have to, I will read your every thought to get the answers I seek.*

*Mako is your master, but you're not from Mares, are you, Zach? You are a Child of Tormenta, aren't you?* Lagos replied, ignoring his comments.

*How about you stop with the question dodging and start talking. Who's the girl in the armor?*

Lagos looked away. *I know nothing about her besides her being the one who caught you.*

*Liar,* Zach replied.

*I beg your pardon?* Lagos demanded.

*You're lying, I know you know her, you've known her for years, I can see it. Hell, you've even trained her!*

*Fine, you're right, I do know her!* Lagos admitted.

*But she's no trainee Watcher, is she?*

182

*No.* Lagos shook his head, still refusing to look at him.

*She's a priestess, isn't she?*

*Azi,* Lagos remarked, using the Wikita word for yes.

*And you are her protector, assigned by the high priestess herself and yet the two of you are so far from home, so I'll ask again. What are you doing here in Mares?*

*The Shanzi, since their return, they set their sights on younger priestesses. As always with war, traitors emerged and put out a hit on her. In order to keep her safe and away from assassins, we had to leave Indiania, but Wikita goblins and sorcerers followed us. I was able to hold them off to start with, but when we washed up here, it became an all-out battle, I was able to cut down the sorcerers, but due to the injuries I had sustained, the goblins were able to take us prisoner and destroy our only means of escape.*

*Then what happened?*

*We found out we weren't alone on this godforsaken land; the goblins who captured us were attacked by another tribe of goblins. Goblins serving a powerful master who was able to destroy the Wikita's leaders and get them to join him; when they did, they gave us over to him. The Goblin King allowed us to live, me to live in this cage, but her, he took her over, filled her head with his hate. Corrupting her as he put her under his spell. She is now his slave, his every wish is her every command.*

*What's her name?*

*Jasmine, Priestess of Celestrial.*

*And how long have you two been on Osiris?*

*A little over two years.*

*And the children?* Zach probes.

*They were here before we were prisoners of the local goblins. To start with there were more of them, but over time, they were fed to the Goblin King.*

*What?* Zach exclaimed in horror.

*They were served as dinner to the King of the Goblins.*

*But it does explain some things.*

*Explains what?*

*In the last thirty-one years, I have been the only child to wash up on the Isle of Iris. I'm Mako's only student and it is our current belief that the children that were meant to arrive at Iris, must have arrived here instead becoming a means of food for this Goblin King.*

*That's why you're here! You've come here to save the children, haven't you?*

*Yes.*

*I take it you had a plan then?*

*I still have a plan,* Zach retorted.

*But you've been captured!*

*I know, but I meant to. Getting captured is all part of the plan.* Zach replied, monitoring the goblins marching around the courtyard. Not one of them was bothering to pay any attention to him.

*What?*

*By getting captured I got brought straight here, put in a cage with the very people I have come to save, which saves me having to find them. Tell me, Lagos, we both know you're not long for this world, we've covered that already, but if I were to put a sword in your hand, could you protect the children and get them to my boat?* Zach asked, looking straight into Lagos' kind green eyes.

*I could, but what is in it for me? What can you offer in return?*

*Jasmine,* Zach said, knowing Lagos' weakness.

*Pardon?*

*I will get Jasmine back for you. I shall destroy this king who has darkened her mind and provide her with safe passage back to the Isle of Iris.*

*You would do that?*

*Azi,* Zach vowed.

*In order to get to the king, you might have to fight her first and regardless of how strong you might be, I doubt you'll be able to beat her without a little help.*

*What kind of help?*

*Jasmine is a very powerful priestess and that's without the powers the king has bestowed upon her. You will need to use magic if you are to beat her.*

*And what do you suggest?* Zach asked.

*A spell. I know a spell that is most effective against her. It will bind her powers, preventing her from using them for a small period of time.*

*For how long?*

*However long you can hold it for. Now I will think the words, but you must not say them because to utter them is to cast the spell, thus activating it. If this occurs and the spell runs out, you will need to wait seventy-two hours before you can use it again.*

*I see.*

*Good. Listen now.* Lagos thought the words, which Zach memorized.

*Got it. Now cover the boys; it's time we break out of here!* He put a hand on the door, grabbing one of the bars, and shook it for all it was worth. The racket attracted the attention of the goblins.

"What's he up to?" One goblin asked another, snarling at Zach.

*Izal!* Zach shouted in thought before yelling, "Hey you! Ugly!"

"Who you calling ugly?" a goblin scowled.

*Izal!* Zach called. "I'm calling you ugly. Ugly!" He mocked.

"Time to teach you a lesson, boy!" the Wikita goblin growled, pulled his keys free, and marched over to the cage.

*Izal!* Zach shouted one last time.

Just as the goblin shoved the key into the lock and

pulled the door open, Zach kicked him right in the face, knocking him backward. Zach quickly stepped out of the cage, ready for battle.

# CHAPTER XXIX:

## *The Battle Begins*

All hell broke loose. Archers readied their bows, goblins on the ground began to charge, and a horn was sounded, announcing the jailbreak. Even so, many goblins weren't sure where to look or what to do. Even though there was confusion everywhere, Zach was the only one who was thinking clearly and was thankful that goblins are stupid.

The first thing he did was rammed the goblin and quickly relieved him of his weapon, cutting him down for good.

*That's one.*

Three goblins ran straight at him, blades drawn, only to stop dead the moment they were within striking distance. The archers had hit the wrong target.

Zach dived to the side and crawled over to a stone column, part of an archway.

*That was close!*

Hearing the heavy breathing of a goblin attempting to sneak up on him, Zach waited until it came around, listening to its every breath before plunging the falchion straight through the abdomen of the goblin with ease.

Yanking his weapon clear, Zach noticed that his defeated opponent was armed with a bow and had a quiver containing a bunch of arrows.

"Now that will come in handy," he remarked.

Choosing to rid himself of the sword, he threw the bloody blade to the ground and snatched up the bow and three arrows. He held them between his four fingers, pulled back on the string, ready to fire all three at once.

*Come on, Izal!* He urged in thought, as more goblins

advanced on his position.

"Where is he?" a brutish voice demanded.

"Anyone got an eyeball?" a second voice called out.

"He's behind the column by the archway!" A third voice shouted, this one belonging to an archer up on the outer wall.

"Anyone with a clear shot?"

"No sir!"

"Not me!"

"Or I!"

"He's all yours!"

"Come on, boys!" one of the more thuggish looking goblins barked.

Zach's breathing stayed slow and controlled as he waited. His eyes were shut, allowing his gift to run wild, enabling him to sense twelve goblins moving in on him and thirteen more up on the outer wall, each one wishing to do him harm. Even though there were many of them, the odds were stacked against them, especially now since he is no longer alone.

*Caw!*

Izal soared overhead, still holding onto Zach's sword. He swooped down repeatedly at the archers, drawing their attention away from Zach.

"Up in the sky!" one goblin shouted.

"A bird!"

"Shoot it!" another ordered.

The raven proceeded to soar upward and circled in front of the sun, preventing the archers from being able to get a clear shot. Zach siezed the moment and let his arrows fly, then ducked under cover to reload the bow.

His arrows flew true, striking their marks cleanly. Three goblins let fly their own arrows, but their aim was wild. One hit nothing at all, one hit a Fori goblin down on the floor, and the third struck down a fellow archer.

Continuing with his assault, Zach fired another two

arrows up at the archers. He would have liked to fire the third one as well, but with four goblins right in front of him, he needed to keep hold of the third arrow to use as a weapon. Holding the arrow like a knife, his eyes studied his four foes, one Wikita goblin, and three Fori each armed with a falchion, but that didn't stop Zach from taking them on. He stabbed the nearest goblin in the kneecap, and sharply kicked him in the face. He then choked a Fori with the bow, dodging a swinging falchion

Zach ripped the arrow out of the first goblin's kneecap and lashed out with it, stabbing a Fori in the throat. The Fori clutched his neck and tried to slow the blood gushing out, only to collapse. Zach stabbed the first Fori in the chest before releasing his grip on the bow. He slammed his elbow down on top of the goblin's head, shattering the bones in his neck.

Zach pulled the arrow out of the Fori, flipped it in his hand, and repeatedly thrust it backward, stabbing the goblin before he slammed his own head backward, breaking the goblin's nose. The Wikita dropped dead.

Turning his attention to the last goblin standing, Zach kicked out repeatedly at him, sending the Fori stumbling backward, grabbed a falchion and made quick work of him.

The remaining armed goblins were surrounding him. Zach stood his ground, then cut loose with a spinning attack, swinging the falchion diagonally from right to left, from up to down. The goblins never had a chance, and fell.

Up until now, the archers had been focusing on attempting to shoot down Izal. Letting Zach live as they preferred not to hit their allies who had him surrounded but he was now open game. They fired arrow after arrow at him. He took advantage of the bodies and used them for cover.

Zach grabbed the biggest Wikita goblin body there was and used it as a shield; what arrows might have hit him, hit the corpse instead. He found good cover, dropped the goblin, and took up the bow.

*Caw!*

*Zach! Are you okay?* Izal continued to fly in circles beneath the sun.

*I'm still alive.*

*Your plan is working.*

*Just be ready to drop my sword.* Zach instructed, yanking some arrows out of his dead friend.

*I'll wait for your cue,* the raven replied.

"Lagos, are you okay?"

"Yes!" Lagos called back.

"Get ready to move!" Zach warned, snatching two arrows out of the corpse and leaping sideways, ditching the cover of the column and firing at the remaining seven goblins.

He fired both arrows and dove back behind cover, only to then snatch up two more arrows, repeating the process until his dead friend had no more to give.

It was time to change tactics. He ran out from behind his protective cover, making sure the archers could see him.

"There he is!"

"Get him!" screamed one of the last three remaining goblins.

"Let 'im 'ave it!" another shouted, and they let their arrows fly.

The goblins were dumbfounded. All of their arrows had missed; each striking nothing but dirt or stone. One second he was there and the next, he wasn't.

Zach stood perfectly still, before he shimmered, and was no longer visible. Within seconds, he reappeared on the outer wall behind the archers.

"He's gone!"

"How?"

*Izal now!*

Izal hurtled down and dropped the sword into Zach's outstretched hand before returning to the sky just as quickly.

"Where is he?" A short, red-skinned goblin asked just before Zach cut him down.

The others were slain before they had time to react. Zach paused, catching his breath.

*Zach!* Izal whooped, landing beside him.

"Izal," Zach bowed his head graciously and cleaned the green blood off his blade, wiping it on the clothes of one of the archers before he sheathed his sword.

*Congratulations on a successful plan,* Izal praised.

"It's not over yet; we still need to get the kids out."

*I know, but still, you have done brilliantly today. I am very proud of you.*

*Thank you, Izal. Now let's get going.* Zach jumped off the wall, and stole a falchion from the carcass of a goblin. Going back to the cage, he took the large set of keys from the goblin who jailed him.

"I told you I'd get you a sword," he remarked as he threw the falchion to Lagos, who had stayed put and watched the whole thing with amazement. "Now, you ready to get out of here?"

"Yes, I am."

"Good. Take these keys and get those kids out of the cages." Zach passed the keys over and gestured to Izal. "Lagos, this is my friend Izal. He is telepathic like me. I want you and the children to follow him. He'll take you straight to my boat."

"And you swear you'll get Jasmine back?" Lagos questioned.

"Lagos, I give you my word."

*Izal, with me.* Zach and Izal left the cage, tasking Lagos to wake the two boys, who had slept through the entire battle.

*You are to get them back to the boat, while I go get*

*Jasmine.*

*This isn't part of the plan, Zach.* Izal cautioned.

*Plans change,* he retorted. *I am getting the girl and there is nothing you can say to change my mind. I will not break my promise to Lagos.*

*But, Zach...*

*But nothing, Izal!* Zach interrupted. *I am doing this!*

*Fine.*

*I'm going to leave you here. There are still goblins in the woods. To make sure you guys get out safely, I'm going to draw their attention away from you all.*

*And how do you intend to do that?*

*With that.* Zach picked up the signal horn.

*I'm not sure about this,* Izal said.

*I'll be fine. Good luck, Izal.*

*You too.*

"Take care, Lagos!" he called out to the older Watcher.

"Same to you, Zach!" replied Lagos.

Zach drew his sword and ran off into the palace, heading straight down a long corridor, conscious of every noise. Even though a thick, red carpet muted the sound of his own steps, he remained attentive to everything. And then he was alone no more.

Jasmine stood before Zach. She adjusted her helmet, and drew her sword, eager to fight.

"Hello, Jasmine, I'm Zach," he greeted in Wikita, hoping to engage the girl in conversation but she remained silent. "I'm here to help. I'm a Watcher, like Lagos. Come with me."

Jasmine ignored his words. She charged him, swinging her sword, wide and out-reaching, displaying lesser experience. Zach effortlessly dodged her every move.

"I don't want to fight you!" Zach yelled, as Jasmine swung at him again. "I'm not your enemy!" He implored.

"Yes, you are. Now fight me, boy!" Jasmine

snarled.

"Fine; have it your way!" Zach retorted, grabbing hold of her right hand and jerking it to one side. He threw a powerful kick to her chest, sending her crashing down. Her helmet came off and her grip on her sword was relinquished. The blade skittered across the stone floor.

Jasmine quickly got to her feet and glared at her opponent. "For that, you will die!"

# CHAPTER XXX:

## *The Battle Rages On*

Jasmine's eyes burned with rage as she snatched up her sword. Zach, however, was as calm as anything, showing no fear. He didn't flinch when she charged straight for him, the blade aimed at his heart.

Instead, he shimmered and vanished, only to reappear to Jasmine's left. He kicked the sword out of her hands and stepped back, moving his own blade against her throat.

"I have no intention of harming you, but if you continue to stand in my way, I'll have no choice but to use force," Zach warned.

"You are an idiot, a true idiot!" Jasmine laughed, her blue eyes turning purple.

"And why is that?" asked Zach, seeing her arming sword levitating off the ground.

"Because I am Jasmine, Priestess of Indiania and the sole daughter of Jasmina, High Sorceress of Celestrial." the young girl boasted proudly, flicking her blond hair.

"And your point is?" replied Zach, aware of the floating sword aimed at his back.

"My point is this, do you honestly believe that you stand a chance against me?" she asked, her nostrils flaring.

"Yes, I do," retorted Zach, spinning quickly and knocking the sword to the floor before he grabbed Jasmine and carried her from one corridor to another of the palace, at full speed.

"What? Where are we?" stammered the surprised priestess, as she tried to make out her surroundings.

"You tell me, you know this place better than I do," Zach said, holding on tighter.

"I will end you!" screamed Jasmine, wrenching

away. Her eyes widened and she immersed herself in magical flames.

"I am not your enemy. I seek only to help you," Zach said softly.

"To help me? I am an all-powerful priestess and you are just a young boy playing Watcher!"

"I am a Watcher who can free you. I can see into your mind and see that you are a slave. The Goblin King may have control over you now, but I can save you from him," Zach said as kindly as he could.

"How can you save me from him? He is everywhere and nowhere. He is the all-powerful, the almighty, and the supreme. No one can harm him. Not even my own magic fazes him!" Jasmine cried as her eyes returned to their natural color and the flames vanished.

"You say that now, but you haven't introduced him to me yet."

"You think you're so tough; you're just a foolish boy. Goblins!" she shouted.

As if summoned by magic itself, more than fifty goblins charged into the corridor, surrounding Zach on all sides. The Fori goblins were armed with thick wooden clubs and the Wikita goblins were equipped with their trusted falchions.

"You summoned us, Lady Jasmine!" growled a tall, slim Wikita goblin.

"This boy seeks to destroy our beloved king. See to it he does not leave this room alive!" Jasmine commanded.

"Yes, Lady Jasmine."

"You're making a mistake," commented Zach, hand on his handle.

"I highly doubt it," retorts Jasmine, turning into a ball of fire and vanishing altogether.

*"Get him!"* commanded the head goblin before the goblins rushed him.

*Fine, everyone dies!* Zach closed his eyes and felt

all of time slow down around him, the goblins included.

When he opened his eyes, he twirled his weapon in his hand, loosening up his muscles. He quickly slashed at the closest foe, stabbed the second closest goblin, and robbed it of its weapon, giving him a second sword to fight with. He could cut them all down, frozen where they stood.

Time soon returned to its natural flow. The dead fell in pieces to the floor, leaving the living charging at each other, none of them realizing that Zach had moved.

"Wait!" a Fori screamed.

"What?" questioned a gruff voiced Wikita.

"He's gone!"

"Where?"

"Right over here!" Zach called out, some ten meters away. The goblins turned in shock.

"Get him!"

"Let's do it!"

Armed with two swords, it was mere child's play for Zach to cut down all those in his way, swinging the blades so fast that they were no longer visible to either species of goblins.

Within seconds, only ten goblins remained standing. One was gifted with a falchion stabbed into its chest, the others followed in turn. A few were stabbed by their own fellows as they tried to keep up with Zach and missed. Standing amongst the dead, Zach suddenly felt a life force coming at him and turned around. He wasn't surprised to see Jasmine, whereas she was very surprised to see him still breathing.

"Hmm, you're still alive," Jasmine scoffed with disgust, as she watched Zach lower his sword, showing no desire to harm her.

"You say that like it's a bad thing."

"I expected the goblins to wipe the floor with you, regardless of how fast you are," Jasmine replied, her voice is cold and course.

"Sorry to disappoint you," Zach replied, turning his back on her and walking away.

"You do not turn your back on me!" Jasmine shrieked.

"I can and I do."

"And just where do you think you're going?"

"To kill the one you call master."

"No, you're not!" Jasmines eyes turned purple once again and she recited a spell. "You've died once already, but now rise up and give your new life to the king you've sworn to serve!"

The dead, even those in several pieces, began to twitch and jerk.

"What?" What's going on?" asked Zach, witnessing the goblins rise again.

"Behold my power, boy; the power of necromancy. The art of bringing the dead back to life! It's beautiful, isn't it? My master taught me this trick!" Jasmine gloated, as the undead circled her and awaited instructions.

"Listen, Jasmine, you're just stalling for time now. The sooner you let me get on and destroy the Goblin King, the sooner I can free you from this spell you're under."

"I tire of your voice. Kill him!"

"And I tire of your games," Zach spat in return.

If live goblins were stupid, undead ones were even more so. Zach repeated his trick and cut them all down in no time, irritated at the waste of energy.

"What magic is this?" Jasmine exclaimed in disgust.

"No magic, just speed," replies the young Watcher. "And now you are going to take me to the Goblin King."

"Or what? Would you kill me if I don't?" Jasmine laughed.

"I made a promise, one that I intend to keep, so no, I'm not going to kill you, but you will take me to him."

Jasmine smiled coyly, holding her hand out for Zach. "Don't fret, young Watcher. I shall do as you wish, but just know that these are your last moments upon this earth."

"We'll see about that," retorted Zach, taking her hand.

"Yes, we will," Jasmine said, and they vanished together.

# CHAPTER XXXI:

## *Enter the Goblin King*

Another day came to an end as they appeared in a corridor outside the throne room. A room with five stained glass windows that let in plenty of light, but over where the black gothic-styled, throne resided, there was no light at all.

What was left of the daylight revealed a thick, purple, bloodstained carpet. The throne was seated in a closed off area, thick drapes blocked it off from sight, shielding it from all light.

The second feature in the room that drew attention was the raised stone platform, a pedestal with three windows magnifying the sunlight into its centre.

Stepping out of a ball of fire in a grand hallway, Zach and Jasmine found themselves standing beside the mahogany double door that led into the throne room. The door was locked from the inside.

"So where's your master then?"

"You have no patience," scoffed a bitterly annoyed Jasmine. She marched over to the double doors and waved her hand, using her powers to unlock them.

"No, I don't," answered Zach, admiring the girl's use of magic. He heard the locks move, the door becoming unbolted. With a second wave of her hand, the priestess blew the doors wide open.

"In you go!" she commanded, beckoning Zach to enter. He complied, his grip on his sword tightening. Jasmine followed him.

"Now what?" Zach asked, seeing closed black curtains shutting off part of the room.

"Now, I lock us in!" she answered, turning and

waving her left hand in front of doors. They slammed shut, the locks fastening.

Zach's senses began to run wild, trying to warn him of impending danger. He felt a huge life force in the room, lurking behind the closed curtains. It awed and frightened him.

"Who dares disturb me?" A loud, malicious, arrogant voice called out from behind the drapes.

Neither Zach nor Jasmine dared say anything. The girl in armor remained silent because she knew better, whereas Zach was quiet because he was trying to get a true measure of the huge power level in the room but he couldn't help but be distracted by the tingling sensation in his arm.

"I said, who dares disturb me!"

"Master Gremora, it is I, Jasmine." She approached the curtain and knelt down. Zach watched her intently.

"And what is your reason for intrusion, my dear Jasmine?" Gremora, the Goblin King bellowed, addressing his servant with a harsh tone that had a touch of affection to it.

"A boy has stormed your fortress, freed your prisoners, and killed all of your guards," Jasmine said humbly, her eyes fixed on the carpet she was kneeling on. Zach however, was wary and stood cautiously near the pedestal of light.

"*What?*" roared Gremora. "Where is this boy?"

Jasmine saw Zach was about to speak, so she looked at him and mouthed no. "He is here, in this very room and he wishes to see you

"And see me he shall." the voice boomed.

The curtains parted, revealing the ugliest, nastiest looking creature Zach had ever laid eyes on. Initially taken aback with shock, he gritted his teeth and stood his ground.

Gremora was huge, his skin pitch black. His feet and hands were enormous, both armed with long, sharp claws. Two long, cruel horns resided either side of his forehead. He had a snubbed nose, the nostrils nothing but large slits. His large mouth was partially open, revealing two massive canines and the rest of his sharp pointed teeth. The gigantic, battle scarred brute wore dark grey armor that covered his torso and abdomen, leaving his massive arms exposed.

But his large black eyes were the worst of it: cruel, malicious, and full of pure hate.

*This is no mere goblin.* Zach told himself. Putting down his fear, he looked directly into the Goblin King's terrifying eyes.

"You have wreaked mayhem in my kingdom, boy! Why?" Gremora probed angrily.

"I came for your prisoners," Zach answered, his voice strong and steady. Jasmine had not moved.

"Why?" Gremora snapped.

"Because they do not belong to you," Zach replied, his voice steady.

"Who are you to say that they do not belong to me?" the Goblin King roared.

"I am Zach, a child of Mantos and I am the one who will bring about your demise!"

Gremora laughed and drew nearer to him. "Mantos, I know Mantos. I destroyed it once, a long time ago."

Zach noticed that the tingling in his arm was starting to sting intensely. He stepped onto the pedestal of light.

"So you think you can destroy me, the Great Gremora, King of the Goblins? Ha! You are a mere ant compared to my might and just like a bug, I will crush you!"

The goblin moved to strike Zach but the sun's rays protected him. The instant sunlight touched the Goblin King's skin it began to burn.

"Argh!" Gremora screamed, pulling it back. What

had been burned to a crisp, was fully restored once back in the shadows.

"Master, are you all right?" Jasmine cried, rushing to her King's aid.

"I'm fine!" Gremora barked, shoving her aside. All of the details came together for Zach. His arm. The name of the Goblin King. The burned and healed hand.

"You're Shanzi!" Zach exclaimed as he realized just who he confronted. "You are Gremora, Shanzi Warlock and servant to Lord Darkari."

"I am a servant to no one, not anymore! I am my own master and the master to the goblins!"

"Well, you're not the Goblin King any more now, are you? I killed all of your followers, most of them twice."

"Grrr!" Gremora growled, enraged. Jasmine stood, and fled to safety.

"Well, it looks like your last follower has deserted you. It's just us now," Zach said.

"I will destroy you, young Watcher. I'll rip your tender flesh from your bones and eat it while you still live. If I feel merciful, I'll rip out your skull and use it as a goblet."

"Sadly for you, Gremora, you will never have that chance." Zach replied, his voice hard-edged.

"But first let's see what you're hiding," Gremora chortled, feeling Zach's memory loss. Believing it to be an attempt to hide certain events, events the Watcher wished the Shanzi not to know, he prepared himself.

"I'm not hiding anything," Zach said through gritted teeth, feeling his presence

"Liar!" the Shanzi growled. He raised his gigantic left hand and fired off a huge bolt of black lightning.

The blast struck Zach head on, hurtling him backward into the stone wall and dropping as if he were a rag doll.

"Ow," Zach groaned weakly, dazed. He felt

something inside his mind—a darkness covering his forgotten memories. Then a sliver of brilliant light pierced it, pried it open, and exploded it.

All of his lost memories played out before him. The memories of Shimay, Mako's doubt, the skills he developed both psychic and physical, all of it came back.

The Goblin King made his way over as Zach picked himself up with his newfound strength.

"Gremora, you have no idea what you have just done and before I kill you, which I will, I must thank you. Thank you for unlocking my memories and reminding me of all the things I can do. Now your time in this world is over."

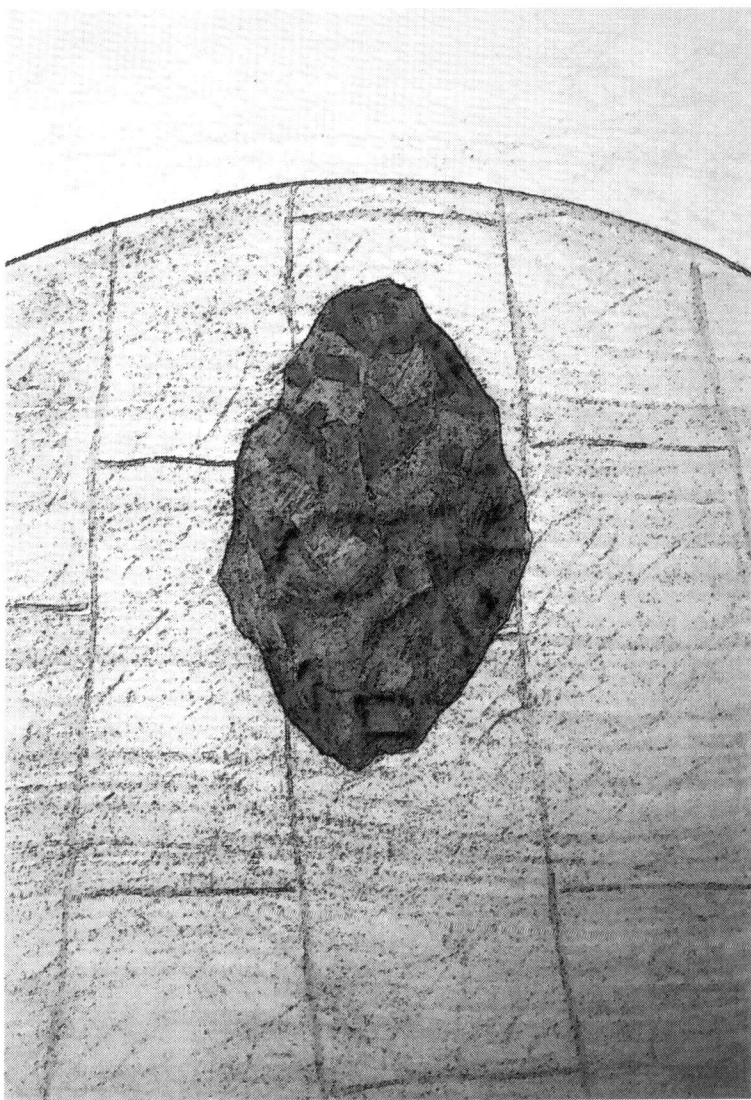

# CHAPTER XXXII:

## *Showdown with a Shanzi*

The Watcher vanished, appearing with his sword in hand, standing protected on a pedestal of light.

"The light won't protect you for long. The sun will soon set and when darkness comes, you are mine," Gremora said. "I can wait. Can you?"

"You're absolutely right, but there's a slight problem with your plan."

"And what's that?"

"You'll be dead before nightfall."

"I am going to enjoy destroying you," Gremora said, charging up an energy ball.

"As am I," Zach said, holding his sword horizontally in front of him.

Gremora threw the bolt. Zach caught it with his sword, electrifying the blade.

"You have some skill," Gremora commented, throwing another ball of black energy at the young Watcher. Zach swung his sword at it. The blade cut through the ball of darkness, sparking an explosion of shadow. The explosion failed to harm Zach, protected by light, but it was more than enough to hurl Gremora into the mahogany double doors.

"Is that the best you can do?" Zach asked.

"How? How did you do that?" Gremora asked, rising warily.

"Thanks to you, I'm seeing a lot of things in my head. Things I had forgotten and things that have taken place since your kind first came to this world."

"That's impossible!"

"Obviously not, but you've got to love the irony. I

am going to kill you now and it is all because of you. You showed me the way to bring about your death."

"Let's see you laugh when I do this!" Gremora exclaimed, firing off three bolts in quick succession, each one stronger than the last. Zach's sword caught them all, storing the energy within the steel.

"Hmm, my turn!" Zach declared, and raised his sword above his head. In a downward slash, the shadow energy burst from the blade, and slammed Gremora to the floor. His armor exploded off him.

Weakened from the blast, Gremora clutched his chest and breathed heavily. "I can see my magic is useless against you and is most effective against myself. Guess I'll have to destroy you by another means." He rose.

Zach saw in his head that Gremora would come at him, engage him in hand to hand. He sheathed his sword and met the Shanzi head on. The two of them went all out, brawling throughout the entire room, doing damage not only to each other but to the room itself.

His first assault felled the Shanzi. When Gremora rose, he blasted Zach into the drapes, tearing them apart as they fell to the floor. Zach threw the throne directly at his enemy, knocking him down.

On they fought. Zach drew on his reserves, gaining new strength as Gremora tired and faltered. Not wishing to extend the fight much longer, he drew his sword and leaping up, he slashed down with all his strength.

"*Aargh!*" Gremora howled. His severed arm slapped the stone floor.

Black blood pumped from what was left of the Goblin King's shoulder. Zach sheathed his sword and took up the arm, holding the huge black hand in his own.

"You took my arm!"

"Yeah, and now I am going to use it against you!" Zach raised the makeshift club and drove Gremora back, closer and closer to the pedestal of light, at last driving him back against it.

"Hey Gremora, fetch!"

As the Shanzi watched in shock, Zach threw the arm onto the pedestal. It landed dead centre in the wash of sunlight, melting away into a black pool of liquid.

"What have you done?"

He never got an answer. Zach caught him with a perfect Midnight Kiss sending the beast falling flat onto the pedestal.

"*No!*" the Shanzi Warlock howled, trapped by the light, and melted away. All that remained of the Dark One was shadow that solidified into a jagged, jet black crystal.

Zach dropped to the stone floor, exhausted and elated at having beaten his first Shanzi. He crawled to the crystal, and picked it up with both hands, only to have the liquid pool of Gremora's arm swirl around his hands and turn into black, fingerless gloves.

The crystal began to leak, the concentrated shadow leaving the jewel, as it seeped into his gloves. Once emptied of darkness, the jewel was now completely transparent.

"What the hell?"

Jasmine burst through the doors.

"Zach!" she called out, her voice full of warmth and concern. There was a great change in her.

"Here!" Zach replied, holding on to the crystal. She ran to him, and enveloped him in a hug.

"I am so glad you're okay."

"It's good to see you too, Jasmine," Zach said, breaking free.

"I am so sorry for the way I was to you, I couldn't help it. Somehow that *thing* was able to put me under some sort of spell that made me serve his every wish, but as soon as you destroyed him, his hold on me was no more." Jasmine smiled.

"I figured," Zach said.

"I'm nothing like that version of me you met. I'm just a polite, kind hearted, down to earth girl who is very gifted when it comes to magic," Jasmine answered.

"Well, in that case, it is nice to meet the *real* you," Zach said, smiling.

"Thank you for saving me," Jasmine said, hugging him again.

"No worries," he replied, starting to walk away.

Jasmine stopped him, and held out her empty hands. As he watched, a rectangular object appeared in them.

"This is for you, a token of my appreciation for saving me," Jasmine said. She gave him a stone tablet made of volcanic rock.

"Thank you, but what is it?" he asked, eyeing the object's details, particularly the two curved lines that met up on the left side.

"I have no idea whatsoever, but whatever it is, it was Gremora's prized possession."

"Well, thanks for the gift. Can you answer me one thing?"

"What?" Jasmine asks, her eyes lighting up with enthusiasm.

"How would you feel about getting out of here and off this island?"

"Lead the way!" Jasmine replied eagerly, and they hurried back to the cave.

# CHAPTER XXXIII:

## *The Return to Iris*

It was now night. Zach and Jasmine made their way back to the smugglers cave and joined the freed prisoners around a lit fire, eating heated soup.

Izal was forced to break the sad news of Lagos' passing. He died fighting a Fori goblin, in defense of the children. Unable to save him, Izal seized the goblin and ripped him to pieces with his sharp talons.

The young girl was shocked and on the verge of tears. Leaving Zach with Izal, she joined the boys around the fire. Although anxious of her, they poured her some soup and offered her bread, and she ate.

*Delfini's are designed for five people and here are nine of you. You, the girl you had to save and the seven prisoners,* Izal said. His keen eyes noticed the tablet and crystal, but he said nothing about them.

"I know, but they are made for five men, we are seven underfed children and one girl. The boat will take their weight and fit them in, I know it." Zach responded.

*And what about you and I?* Izal probed.

"You're flying us back to Iris tonight!"

*You sense something is wrong, don't you?* Izal asked, reading the worry in Zach's head.

"Mako is in trouble; at least he will be if we don't get there in time."

*Then we will leave. But what about them? How will they find Iris if we leave them?*

"With a little help from a friend." Zach walked over to the water's edge and called out. *Fluke?*

*Here!* the dolphin replied, surfacing close to Zach.

*Izal and I need to return to Iris tonight and I was*

*hoping if you could do me a massive favor and help guide the children to the Isle of Iris?*

*You were able to get them out? You're incredible! Is there anything you can't do?* Fluke squeaked happily.

*I wouldn't go that far, but I do need your help with the children.*

*Of course I will help them reach your island.* Fluke replied, more than happy to aid Zach once again. *In fact, I'll get my whole pod to help out. We'll be much quicker that way.*

*Thank you, Fluke. I appreciate your assistance. Be ready to leave in one hour.*

*We will.* Fluke grinned toothily, and then swam off to gather his fellow dolphins.

Zach walked over to Jasmine.

"Hey," he said.

"Hey yourself."

"Izal and I need to depart for Iris right away, so we can get things ready for your arrival. Will you be all right to sail everyone back in my boat? You've just got to head west."

"I know how to sail, but I don't know these waters."

"I figured you'd say that, which is why my dolphin friends are going to help you get there."

"Well, if we've got a dolphin escort to guide us, then I should have no problems sailing the boat," Jasmine smiled.

"Good. Be ready to leave in one hour."

"Hey, Zach?"

"Yeah?"

"Is there something you're not telling me?" She asks suspiciously.

"No, nothing." he lied, thinking of Shimay. He joined Izal.

"Let's go."

They soared through the night sky for the next four

hours. Reaching Iris in record time, they noticed smoke rising from the chimney and headed straight for the house on the volcano.

"Mako!" Zach called, running into the house.

"Zach!" Mako exclaimed, coming down the stairs.

"Thank goodness you're all right!"

"Of course I am. Glad you are as well."

"I thought Shimay might have attacked you, now that he's free."

"What are you talking about?"

*Hello, Mako,* the raven greeted upon entry.

*Hello, Izal.*

"Shimay; he's escaped," Zach repeated.

*You've felt this?* Izal exclaimed.

"No, I saw it," he answered, placing the crystal and tablet down on the table.

"You had a vision?" Mako asked.

"Yes."

*Since when did you have visions?* "I started having them the day Shimay tried to kill me and then I stopped due to the memory loss, but since my showdown with Gremora..."

"Gremora?"

*As in the Shanzi warlock?* Izal questioned.

"Yeah, him. He foolishly unlocked my memories and a whole lot of other stuff, like new powers and visions of past events before I killed him."

*You killed a Shanzi Warlock?*

"Yeah, it was easy really. I beat him with his own severed arm and forced him backward into concentrated sunlight, which made all of him melt into dark goo that congealed into this crystal." Upon mentioning the jewel, Zach held it up for the others to see. "I guess when he unlocked my memories, he must have unlocked a more sadistic side of me too."

"Let me see that crystal!" Mako snapped, snatching

the jewel from his student's gloved hands.

Mako studied the transparent crystal, looking worried. "Was this black before you touched it?"

"Yes, why?"

*Do you know what this is?*

"Not really."

"It's a Shanzi crystal. When a higher classed Shanzi is destroyed, they turn into crystals, much like this one. It is their power solidified into an object that can be passed onto another." Mako set the jewel back down on the table.

*Where did you get those gloves?* Izal probed, eyeing them warily.

"When I picked the crystal up, the goo leaked out and covered my hands, becoming gloves that absorbed everything."

"And can you take them off?" Mako inquired.

"Dunno, let me check," Zach lowered his gaze and removed them easily. "Does that answer your question?"

*Thank Tormenta for that!* Izal exclaimed.

"Why? What's wrong?"

"Shanzi crystals can be very, very dangerous, Zach," Mako said. "There have even been some cases where some crystals have possessed whoever touched them and then there are ones that pass over magical powers. One theory is that magic only came into being because of the Shanzi crystals, but regardless of whether they do or they don't, they are still very dangerous and can change a person completely."

"How so?"

Izal drew nearer, and looked into his eyes.

*When I was a young man, I ignored Mako's wishes and touched one of his black Shanzi crystals. The result is what you see now, a man transformed into a Shanzi raven.*

"You used to be human!" Zach exclaimed, deeply shocked.

*I used to be, a long time ago.*

216

"I never knew."

"And that, Zach, is exactly why you should never touch a Shanzi crystal with bare hands. It is also why you should never wear these gloves. There is no way of knowing what they will do to you."

"I understand." He nudged the items away. "So what is this?" he asked, gesturing to the tablet.

Mako and Izal glanced at each other, recognition filling their faces.

"It is a stone tablet made of volcanic rock, one of three which, when gathered together, are assembled into a key, which..."

Zach finished for him. "Which is used to unlock the sacred seal to the Shanzi temple inside the volcano below us."

"Exactly right. Now, how about you bring me up to date? Where are the children you went to rescue? How did you even find Gremora?"

Zach filled him in, concluding, "As for the children, they are safe and sound, currently en route to Iris aboard the Delfini, being escorted by a pod of dolphins."

"Dolphins?"

"Yeah, dolphins. When we were heading to Osiris we came across a dolphin in trouble and helped him out. Afterward, Fluke felt grateful for my help, so, eager to repay me, he had his pod help get us to Osiris much quicker. Still wishing to thank us, Fluke stuck around all day and was more than eager to help again by escorting the Delfini.

"You're telling me that the children you went to save are now at sea and that you have left them all alone with dolphins?"

"Yeah."

"Izal?"

*Yes, Mako?*

"Do me a favor; fly out and meet the boat. I would

feel a lot better knowing you were with them."

*Of course.* Izal stepped through the doorway and took flight.

Alone with his mentor, Zach spent the next few minutes filling Mako in on every detail of the first half of his quest. Starting from setting off, he got up to his second run-in with Jasmine, only to be interrupted by something he felt.

A tremendous power was rising, coming from outside the house.

"We need to get out of here, now!" He grabbed Mako and they fled just as Shimay threw a huge shadow energy ball at the house, blasting it apart with a catastrophic *boom.*

# CHAPTER XXXIV:

## *Return of the Spirit*

Laying half-conscious on the hard surface of the crusted over volcano, Zach tried to shake off the impact and assess his immediate surroundings. Debris was everywhere, the house and its contents shattered save for a few weapons lying about. What he couldn't find was Mako. He pushed himself up off the ground and stood up, looking in every direction as a shooting pain filled his left arm.

"Zach! I thought I killed you and yet here you are, still breathing," the demented spirit sneered.

"Never say die!" Zach replied, using the phrase from his dream.

"Never say die, I'll remember that one, but tell me, Zach, how did you survive my attack?" Shimay's sharp teeth glistened brightly.

Zach carefully stepped back, drawing his sword, and feeling out for Mako's life force. His mentor lay unconscious under a shield some ten meters away.

"You're not going to answer me?" Shimay sneered, his pale hands wrapping themselves around an axe.

"I didn't answer because I don't know," Zach said coldly.

"I guess some things are best left unanswered. Besides, this way I have the pleasure of killing you all over again and this time I will not fail." He swung the axe. Zach avoided it, stabbing Shimay in the arm.

Thick, black blood flowed at first; within seconds, it stopped. The wound began to heal.

Zach watched in horror, thinking fast.

"Fascinating, isn't it? Before, you could hurt me, but now, now when my powers have grown even more so, your sword is now useless as now my ability of self-healing is second to none."

"You know what, Shimay?"

"What?"

"You talk too much." Zach grabbed a spear and threw it at the spirit, knowing that he would dodge to his right. Zach darted in, cutting Shimay to ribbons before distancing himself from his enemy.

"That's a decent tactic you used, Zach, and for that you win back your life for a few more minutes."

Standing near the rim of the volcano, Zach started to move.

He was too late. Shimay acted quickly and blasted him backward, over the edge.

*The blast and the fall will not kill you, but by the time you recover, Mako will be dead.*

Mako was starting to come to as Shimay drew near. The spirit snatched him up by the front of his tunic and looked straight into his eyes.

"Hello, Mako," Shimay said, gloating.

"Iris! What have you done with Zach?"

"First of all, it's Shimay. Second, I wouldn't worry about Zach. If I were you, I'd be far more concerned about myself."

"I'm not afraid of you." To prove his point, Mako whipped one hand up and jabbed Shimay in the eyes.

Shimay dropped him and staggered back, howling in pain. Mako leaped to his feet and charged, sword in hand. The sword glided straight through Shimay, emerging from his back.

Shimay grabbed the blade and pulled it free. "This island is full of idiots!" The horrible injury began to heal immediately. "You stabbed me! Now that's not very nice, is it?"

Mako saw a battle axe nearby and grabbed it just in time to fend off Shimay's relentless sword attacks. His mind and body were one: fluid, focused, and deadly.

"Had enough?" Mako asked, taunting him.

"You dare mock me!"

"You deserve it," Mako replied.

"You are an insignificant bug, your power is nothing compared to mine!"

"That may be so, but I'm still alive, aren't I?"

"You remain breathing purely because I allow you to live."

"Then what are you waiting for?"

"Good question," the spirit replied, throwing Mako's long sword at him. Mako bent to catch it, glancing down for the briefest of seconds.

When he looked up, the energy ball flung him skyward, driving him back down to the ground. Mako lay gasping, the wind knocked out of him, pain taking the place of air.

"You made me do that." Shimay went over to him and tutted "What's the matter Mako, tired of playing?"

"If you're going to kill me, just do it already," groaned Mako, looking up at the night sky filled with stars and a bright full moon.

"Now *that* is an idea." He charged up another energy ball, preparing to end it all.

The energy ball was never released. Shimay raised his arm to fling it, only to have his severed hand fall to the ground.

"I'm here, Master, and I shall finish this!" Zach vowed.

"Zach, no!" Mako shouted.

Fuelled with determination, Zach engaged Shimay. The two dueled vigorously, each eager to cut down their opponent.

Mako could do nothing but look on in horror. Unable to help his student, he drew up the last tatters of his strength.

Finding his long sword, Mako leaped to Zach's aid, forcing Shimay to take on the both of them, but with every injury he sustained, Shimay quickly healed. Mako knew something else had to be done.

"We should retreat, Zach! Our swords have no effect!"

"Then we change tactics!" Refusing to give in, Zach telepathically transmitted a new plan.

Fighting in sync, the two of them forced Shimay backward, causing him to stumble repeatedly and at last go down on the rocky ground. Both swordsmen plunged their blades into him, trapping the spirit in place. Under their steel, Shimay's form shimmered, lost solidity, and turned into a cloud of shadow. For only a moment, his voice remained, filling the air.

"Fools! The both of you! I am Shimay, son of Shanzi and I am your destruction!"

With a full moon lurking above, moonbeams bathed down upon the land, merging the shrouded shadow, solidifying it into Shimay's reborn form. Transforming him into a being; tall, slender, beautiful, blacker than the night sky.

Shimay stepped forth out of the moonlight and pounced toward Zach and Mako.

# CHAPTER XXXV:

## *Shimay's True Form*

"**B**eautiful, aren't I?" Shimay asked, flexing his limbs.

Zach was stunned, as the pain in his arm intensified, whereas Mako was not surprised in the slightest, having known the truth about Shimay all along. His master had become one with their mortal enemy.

No longer a demonic looking humanoid, Shimay was now much shorter and very slim. His crescent shaped eyes moved skyward, noting incoming rain.

Zach moved to charge, only to have Mako halt him.

*No, Zach! Wait.*

*For what? He's Shanzi, we've got to destroy him.*

*I agree, but it's night time, the advantage is his. Without sunlight, we have no means of destroying him.*

*Then we must keep him here until sunrise. By any means necessary,* Zach replied, full of conviction.

Lowering his gaze from the sky, Shimay turned to Mako and his disciple, determined to finish what he started.

*I agree, Zach, but I do this alone. Unless I fall, stay out of this.*

*What?*

"Shimay?" Mako called out.

"Yes, Watcher?"

"Let's end this, right now. I challenge you to a one-on-one. To the death. Do you accept?" Mako challenged.

Shimay's answer came in the form of a sudden attack, not on Mako but Zach, blasting him away before he pounced on his challenger.

Rain began to fall as Mako and the Shanzi battled it out, each one resorting to fists and weapons. Despite heightened speed and power, Shimay found himself overwhelmed by the Watcher. It was time to turn the tables.

Mako proved to have the advantage on the ground so Shimay took the battle to the air, hurling Mako upward.

Overwhelmed and close to total exhaustion, Mako knew he was close to his end, unable to defend himself against any of Shimay's multiple kicks and punches. Each one caused him unbearable pain, but he continued.

Despite his efforts, it was no good; Shimay's blows kept hitting home and worse yet, Mako knew it was all a game to the Shanzi. The Dark One was holding back.

"You're not looking too good, Mako!" he taunted, following his comment with another punch, sending Mako upward again. "I expected more from you."

Thrown to the ground, Mako groaned in agony as Shimay stood above him, charging two energy balls.

Zach lurked on the other side of the volcano caldera. He wished to run over and prevent the impending act, but Shimay held out an energy ball as a warning.

"You are pitiful, Mako, you always have been. To think you believed you could stop me, what a joke!"

"No, Shimay, the joke is on you if you think you can defeat Zach. I know now what he is, what he can do," he said, having full conviction in his student.

"Is that so?" Shimay replied.

With both balls fully charged, the time for Mako's destruction had come.

Zach knew his current speed was no match for Shimay's and that an attempt to save his mentor would be pointless, unless he were to break the vow he took.

*I couldn't, could I?*

Mako heard him. *It's okay, Zach. If I must die so you shall live, so shall it be. Destroy him, Zach, for both of us.* One second Mako was about to succumb to death; the next he was carried to safety and laid to rest at the other end of the volcano. Zach stood over him as his accelerated heart raced.

"Get some rest, Master, I'll handle this."

"How dare you!" Shimay howled in raw fury, frustrated to have his desire denied.

Speeding over to Shimay, Zach scorned at the Dark One in his presence.

"You had no right to intervene!"

"I had every right. It is my fault we are in this mess and it is me who will put it right."

"You dare challenge me?" Shimay laughed.

"Yeah, I do," he replied, leaping into action.

# CHAPTER XXXVI:

## *All or Nothing*

Shimay was instantly overwhelmed by Zach. No matter how much stronger he had become, he knew Zach to be more so.

No matter what he tried to do, the young Watcher would easily get through his defenses and bring the pain.

The only way the Shanzi could see himself besting Zach was if he engaged in a new tactic. One featuring the element of surprise.

With his heightened senses, Zach already knew that Shimay who was no match for him, not when he was using the Advanced Blood Rush. However, all his strength and speed didn't count for anything during the nocturnal hours because until the sun rose, he had no means of vanquishing the Shanzi.

All he could do was just keep on fighting until the morning light came.

"Wait!" Shimay called out.

Zach's latest sword attack paused in mid-swing.

"Why?" he asked.

"You know as well as I do this is pointless. Besides, it doesn't have to be this way. You and I can be one!" the Dark One said.

"What, like you and Iris?"

"No, Zach, not like Iris and I, for we would be so much greater."

"Yeah, no thanks."

"Just think about it, Zach! We could be the greatest being ever to exist!"

"You mean the greatest Shanzi ever to exist."

Shimay knew he would get nowhere with Zach, that

the young Watcher would never join with him, but his plan wasn't about Zach. Sure, it would have been a welcome bonus, but it was merely a ploy to distract the Watcher from the Dark One's true plan.

With burning hate, Zach unleashed another onslaught upon Shimay, hacking away, before a thought occurred to him.

It was all well and good to just keep attacking, but if Shimay is so keen to talk, then why not talk? It would help pass some time.

"Just tell me one thing, why? Why are you doing this?"

"Power, Zach, power!" Shimay answered. "I was a low level Shanzi, a speck of evil compared to the rest, but then a weak Child of Tormenta came along. He was desperate to make a name for himself, so we made a deal, fusing together to become something much stronger."

"You corrupted him!" Zach snapped.

"No, Zach, I helped him! I helped him kill many of my own kind and rid the Mares Realm of Lord Darkari. It was I who opened the portal that banished the Shanzi King."

"But why? What did you get out of your sordid deal?"

"His soul."

"His soul, why? What's so special about it?"

"By getting his soul, the two of us could never be separated. In life, or in death, which is why when you first met me I had a human form, but due to what Iris' spirit became after fusing with me, his soul took on a more demonic appearance."

"There was another reason why you wanted his soul, wasn't there?" Zach asked. "What was it that his soul was able to do for you?"

"It had allowed me to cheat the death I knew I would eventually face, for I, like the rest of my kind, were doomed. We were losing the war against the Watchers, so I did what I had to for my kind!"

"That's why you did it, not to save my world, but to save your kind, to remove them from a world where they stood no chance, only to bring them back centuries later when the Watchers had dwindled. Locking them away to cheat death."

"You got it in one, boy," Shimay snarled.

"But you couldn't do it, could you? You couldn't open the portal because you didn't have the power to do it, did you?"

"You're right; I couldn't do it, despite many years of trying. I just wasn't strong enough. So fifty years ago, I left the temple and started living in the forest, starting my quest for power."

"It wasn't just Gremora was it? You were also responsible for..." Zach stammered, unable to finish his sentence.

"Mako only having the one student in the last thirty-one years? Yes, I am. Originally I would let him find most of the ones that made it, only taking one for myself every couple of months, but absorbing one baby's life force at a time, it wasn't enough. So for the last thirty-one years I took them all, feeding on all of Mako's potential students and you all tasted so good. Babies really are a Shanzi's favourite meal."

"You're...you're sick! You Shanzi are all the same, you and Gremora may look different, but you're exactly the same!"

"You keep saying that. Why do you keep going on about that old waste of space warlock?"

"Because I've met him, over on Osiris Island."

"Gremora, he's alive! I should have known!" Shimay cursed. "If I had, then my plans of restoring Lord Darkari and the others would have come to fruition ages ago."

"Yeah, well, Gremora will be no help to you now. I made sure of it."

"You killed your first Shanzi. Bravo, Zach. Bravo. I knew I was right to let you live. To let you grow up, get strong, strong enough to help develop my own powers before I could then absorb yours. You made me great, but it was Mako who played his part brilliantly; only he had the ability to banish me into the temple where I was able to use those powers you gave me, to carry out my plan."

"What do you mean?" Zach demanded.

"When I escaped the temple tonight, I didn't escape alone. I brought a few friends along with me."

"What?"

"So you see, Zach, it doesn't matter if you destroy me, I have already won. There is nothing you can do to stop us."

This was it, Shimay's perfect moment to strike. With Zach stunned, it was the perfect time to deliver his killer blow.

Energy balls weren't his only devastating attack, for Shimay possessed something much greater. With a quick whipping motion of the hand, Shimay let loose a huge lightning bolt.

The blast hit Zach and sent him backward, crashing to the ground. For a moment, he laid there, his body twitching from the shock, his face to the moonlight.

*That's it!*

With a pause in his torture, he got to his feet slowly, sword in hand. His enemy watched him with amusement.

"Hey, Shimay!" he called, thrusting his sword skyward. "I call upon Lucifer, the Morning Star! Bestow your rays upon my blade so I may smite this Shanzi foe!"

"Really, Zach, have you forgotten you need sunlight to make that work?"

"Now that's where you're wrong, Shimay! I don't need direct sunlight to destroy you. Not when reflected sunlight will do, so that full moon that empowers you will also be the end of you!"

Proving him right, the sword lit up with a silver glow, the light from the moon engulfing the blade.

"This is goodbye, Shimay."

"So what! Darkari and his followers shall soon be here. You won't stop my kind! They will destroy your world, taking all of you with it!"

Zach charged at Shimay in a full out advanced Blood Rush, his sword now easily hacking the Shanzi apart before he rammed the point home.

Silver light filled Shimay, burning him as it flared bright before he suddenly exploded. Caught by the shock wave, Zach was hurled backward, striking his head on stone and the world went black.

# CHAPTER XXXVII:

## *Sunrise on Iris*

The downpour of rain had long ceased. The darkness fled in the light of a new day dawning.

Mako sat on the ledge overlooking Dead Man's Beach, resting a hand on his injured hip. Still in a lot of pain, he was recovering from the previous night's exertions.

Zach lay passed out next to him, alive and breathing. His clothes had changed, the colors now black and dark grey.

With a sharp intake of breath, Zach's eyes opened and he sat up, his eyes adjusting to the brilliant light. He found Mako looking at him.

"Hey," Zach smiled happily, pleased to see his master still alive. "We're not dead, are we? This isn't heaven, is it?"

Zach's comment made Mako burst out in laughter.

"No, Zach, we are still among the living."

Zach moved to hug his tutor, only to see Mako shake his head.

"How are you feeling?" Zach asked, genuinely concerned.

"I'm a bit banged up, but I've had worse," Mako said, playing down his pain.

"So where's Shimay? He is dead right?" Questioned the youthful blue-eyed Watcher, unable to recollect how his clash with the Dark One ended.

"Shimay is well and truly destroyed. Your tunic is proof of this fact," he answered, motioning his student to take a look at himself.

Zach obliged with no delay.

"What happened to my tunic?"

"Shimay did." Mako answered, but judging by the puzzled look on Zach's face, he knew he needed to explain further. "When you pierced his chest with the moonlight stored in your sword, it destroyed him, turning him into a cloud of shadow and without sunlight to solidify the shadow into a crystal, it was absorbed by the fabrics of your uniform. It even created the sleeves you now bear."

"So Shimay's gone; we won?" Zach asked.

"Yes and no. We haven't won, Zach, we haven't won anything. Last night you destroyed two extremely powerful Shanzi, which is a great thing, but Shimay was able to aid a few of his kind in getting out of the temple and off the island. There is no way of knowing just how powerful they are, or where they are. Worse still, he's also been able to re-open the portal, which means that Lord Darkari can now return."

"So I messed up," Zach said glumly, bowing his head in shame.

"Not at all," Mako grinned. "In fact, you did great. Last night you battled two Shanzi and you destroyed them both, and more importantly, Gremora was Darkari's right hand Shanzi, his most powerful soldier. With him destroyed, Darkari will no longer be able to use him for his magical gifts or his evil knowledge. Besides, just because there are more Shanzi in the world now and Darkari is going to return, not all is lost because I now know that you are the one who will destroy them all. Your powers continue to grow every day. It is the Shanzi who are no match for you, or your relentless determination."

"That may be true, but there's a reason Shimay wanted Darkari back. I am nowhere near strong enough to take him on."

"From what I saw last night, I highly doubt that. You have a lot more power than you know and with regards to Darkari, even if you're not ready for him now, we've got four years to prepare you for him."

"Why four years? Surely he'd want to return sooner now that the portal is open?"

"Darkari is clever. He will not step foot in this world while there is still a potential threat--us. This is why Shimay helped the other Shanzi to escape, because they are the first wave."

"The first wave?"

"Yes, their task is simple, to infiltrate our world, to blend in and observe our defenses. For three years they will do nothing but watch."

"But why?"

"Our world has changed a lot since their last visit; they will need to reassess everything they know about us before the time comes for them to attack, and attack they will. The ones Shimay helped escape will wreak havoc in the Mares Realm in a bid to get us to abandon our post, allowing Darkari and his followers safe passage out of the temple because we would not be here to stop them."

"So, what? We are to let the Shanzi take over Mares while we remain here waiting for Darkari and the rest to come? We should go after the others now, take them out while we still can!" Zach cried out, eager to fight.

"Sadly, it is not that easy, Zach. Even with the mark upon your arm, finding the freed Shanzi is nigh impossible. For the next three years, they will mask themselves most brilliantly, truly blending into our world. To even try looking for them would take far too many years, years best suited to training."

"Then what are we supposed to do?"

"We wait, Zach. We wait for the Shanzi to expose themselves. Then, and only then, will you set out to take care of them, whereas I will remain here to watch over the temple in your absence. Then when you return, we will take Darkari together."

"Well, if I am to fight him, just who is he? Both you and Shimay have mentioned him, but you've never actually explained him, or his story."

"Darkari is a story I will tell you, but now is not the time for it."

"Well, what about you being 253 years old? Can we talk about that?" the boy probed, as he watched Mako's facial expression very carefully. "How are you still alive?"

Letting out a deep sigh, Mako bowed his head. He knew this day would come eventually.

"I'm not like you," he answered.

"What do you mean?"

"I am only partially alive, a living ghost, if you will. The truth is I died a long time ago."

"On the night you fought with Iris, he wasn't the only one to die that night, was he?"

"No, he wasn't. Iris was infected with the Shanzi you knew as Shimay and I wished to set him free of his curse, so we battled. In our duel, I was able to overpower him, delivering a deadly blow that would result in him bleeding to death."

"So why did you lock him away in the temple?"

"Because I had no other choice. He was becoming Shanzi and when we clashed, it was nighttime. If he were to die outside, his Shanzi form would have risen, and begun his plan to let loose the Dark Ones and take control of our world. With it being night, there would have been nothing I could do to stop him."

"So you locked him in the temple, so when his human side died, Shimay would be trapped until he discovered a way to escape," Zach surmised, putting two and two together.

"Exactly right. Now, because I've answered your question, maybe you can answer something for me?" Mako looked out to sea and Zach did the same.

"Sure."

"How the hell did you know how to destroy Shimay with a full moon?" Mako exclaimed. Until he witnessed it himself, he did not know such an act was possible.

"I had a vision of a Watcher doing exactly the same thing, using the full moon to destroy a Shanzi and I just went with it." What Zach didn't admit was that the Watcher he saw in the vision was the same man he saw in his recurring dream.

"Well, I'm glad you did, Zach. After all, it paid off, but we do have to discuss you using the advanced Blood Rush technique again."

"Do we have to?" Zach protested.

"Yes, we do. You've used it three times now, the third time lasting a lot longer than your first two."

"I know, but I had to. It was the only way," replied Zach, justifying his use of it.

"I believe you, Zach, and that is why I revoke what I said to you that day in the forest. You use it better than any Watcher ever has and I now know that you can handle it, but please remember unless you are Elohim, it is very dangerous, and it will kill you if you overdo it. Therefore I would like you to promise me that you'll only use it if you absolutely have to." Mako's voice was gentle and serious.

Nodding his head straight away, Zach laid his hand on Mako's. "I swear."

"Good." Mako breathed a sigh of relief.

"You never said how you died."

"You're quite right. Well, it happened in the temple. I believed Iris to be out cold, but as soon as I turned my back on him, he ran me through with my own sword. The wound didn't kill me right away. I was able to leave the temple and I died in the open just as the sun rose. Except my soul did not pass on. The Isle of Iris must have a Guardian, a dedicated protector to defend the Mares Realm and prevent the Shanzi from breaking free. Therefore, my soul is forever bound to Iris, never to age and never to leave. For the most part, I remain mortal. I can be hurt, feel pain, eat, laugh, cry, but I can never leave this island. You see, Zach, I am the true Spirit of Iris."

"That makes perfect sense, actually," Zach responded. He lay back on the grass, looking up at the cloud free sky. "I can't believe the house is destroyed," he murmured.

"Neither can I, but we can rebuild it. We've got all the supplies we need and the time," Mako said, his eyes on the sea.

"Well, we'll have to make it bigger than before, now that we'll have a lot more company," Zach replied, thinking about Jasmine and the other children he saved from Gremora and the goblins over on Osiris.

"Well, at least there will be plenty of extra hands to help with the work and speaking of extra hands..." Mako tapped Zach's leg.

Zach stood up with his master and smiled. Out on the water was a Delfini, its sails raised, and children its cargo. Izal flew above the boat, keeping it on course, and Fluke and his pod surrounded it, protecting it.

"It appears we have company," commented a grinning Mako.

*Caw!*

Zach turned to Mako and grabbed him by the hand. "Come on, we can meet them on the beach!" Zach urged.

"Why don't you go on ahead? I'll be down in a bit."

Zach smiled and hurried off.

Shaking his head with joy, Mako watched as Zach began to laugh from sheer exultation. As much as he too wanted to be joyous, Mako couldn't help but have a dark thought.

*I hope you enjoy this day, Zach. Soon the days of true darkness will come and then the real fight will begin.*

Smiling, Mako went down to the beach to meet them.

# Here ends Book I of the *Rise of the Elohim Chronicles*

## About the Author:

I'm Rocky Rochford, an early twenties author born and bred in the UK. Instead of living life in cold, wet England, I currently reside in Spain, where I have lived for the past decade. Based on my first novel, and the first book in the Deep Water (Phoenix Rises) series, an espionage/thriller novel , fueled by Royal Navy Captain John Herman Lewis' strong desire for revenge.

Not content with just novel writng, my background features various activities. For the last ten years, I've taken to freelance journalism in addition to being a columnist. I've completed a book of poetry and penned a screenplay for a music academy.

Scuba is another love close to my heart, as is conversation, leading me to become a trained PADI Divemaster. Jacques Cousteau is one of my idols and always will be.

## Acknowledgements:

Firstly I would like to make my first thank you to the talented illustrator, Ashleigh Longman, who I had the great pleasure of working with as she Illustrated this novel. Without her hard work and long hours spent on each and every drawing, this book would not have been the same and it is also for that reason that I also dedicate this book to you.

I also want to thank my supporting family, the brother who got me back in the writing seat, the mother who reads my every works, my father who taught me the value of self-reliance and never giving in.

Lastly I want to thank Solstice Publishing for making the dream of seeing this book through to the end, become a reality. I'd also like to thank each and every reader for without you, writers would have no one to share their creativity with.

Enjoy.

## Social Media Links:

Twitter: https://twitter.com/RockyRochford

Facebook: https://www.facebook.com/IamRockyRochford?ref=ts&fref=ts

Website: http://rockyrochford.ronpelt.com/

Made in the USA
Charleston, SC
29 September 2014